Cara Summers

SEXY SILENT NIGHTS

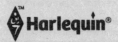
Harlequin®

TORONTO NEW YORK LONDON
AMSTERDAM PARIS SYDNEY HAMBURG
STOCKHOLM ATHENS TOKYO MILAN MADRID
PRAGUE WARSAW BUDAPEST AUCKLAND

Recycling programs
for this product may
not exist in your area.

ISBN-13: 978-0-373-79659-5

SEXY SILENT NIGHTS

ABOUT THE AUTHOR

Was Cara Summers born with the dream of becoming a published romance novelist? No. But now that she is, she still feels her dream has come true. And she owes it all to her mother, who handed her a Harlequin romance novel about fifteen years ago and said, "Try it. You'll love it." Mom was right! Cara loves writing for the Blaze line because it allows her to create strong, determined women and seriously sexy men who will risk everything to achieve *their* dreams. When she isn't working on new stories, she teaches in the writing program at Syracuse University and at a community college near her home.

Books by Cara Summers

HARLEQUIN BLAZE

To get the inside scoop on Harlequin Blaze and its talented writers, be sure to check out blazeauthors.com.

All backlist available in ebook.

To my nephew Nick and my new niece Kristen.
May all your future Christmases together be merry!
And especially to my great-nephew Luca—
who celebrates his very first Christmas this month.

I love all three of you!

1

One sexy silent night...5:00 a.m.

CILLA MICHAELS WAS NOT GOING to leave the hotel room without her panties. She'd been a cop for three years, a private security agent for two, and now she headed up G.W. Securities' new office in San Francisco. She was a pro at tracking things down.

On her hands and knees, she inched her way quietly down the length of her side of the bed, using her hand to sweep the space beneath it as she went.

Nothing.

She was not the kind of woman who would abandon anything that had a La Perla label on it. She'd parted with a small fortune for the red lace bikini, and it was part of a set. The matching camisole had already been located near the nightstand. She had a vague recollection of stripping it off and tossing it there herself. While in the throes of uncontrollable passion. Because that's exactly what Jonah Stone had sparked in her.

Ducking her head down, she lifted the dust ruffle and peered beneath. The dim light slipping through the narrow slits in the drapes didn't provide much in the way of illumination.

The rest of her clothes she'd found quite easily near the door of the hotel suite where Jonah Stone had efficiently stripped her out of them. The man had fast moves, and just thinking about what had happened the instant the door had closed behind them brought back the sensation of those hard hands on her skin, the impatience, the demand. And the pleasure.

Heat shimmered through her, pooling in her center and then radiating outward. He'd taken her the first time right there. No small talk. No talk at all. But the foreplay had been top-notch. His hands had pushed into her hair, and she'd felt each of those hard, slender fingers while he'd assaulted her mouth with lips, teeth and tongue. Each sensation had been so sharp. If she lived to be a hundred, she would never forget his mouth, his taste.

Then he'd moved those hands over her shoulders, shoving her jacket off and molding her body with such purpose and skill.

He'd smelled so good and felt better—hard and tough and male. Hadn't she been imagining him just like this ever since the instant she'd first seen him at that party yesterday?

When those smoky-gray eyes had collided with hers, something had clicked inside of her like a switch turning brains cells off and lust on—full throttle. That was the only explanation she could come up with for agreeing to his one-night stand proposition.

His argument had been logical enough—just the kind you'd expect from an astute businessman. After all, they were unattached adults, intensely attracted to each other, and fate in the form of an airport-closing blizzard had thrown them together. Why not pleasure each other for one long, sexy night and then go their separate ways?

She might have come up with at least two good reasons why not. In fact she'd been thinking about them when he'd suddenly appeared at her table in the lounge of the hotel. But looking into his eyes had triggered that little click again, and sent logic flying.

That was how she'd ended up against the door of his hotel room, his mouth branding hers. She had only a blurry recollection of how her sweater and slacks had hit the floor. Her focus had been on those hard hands moving up her legs and heating her blood to the boiling point. She'd never before experienced such intense sensations. Never wanted anyone so desperately. He'd opened up a new and wonderful world for her. Sensations flooded through her again as she recalled how he'd slipped fingers beneath the thin lace that still covered her, pushed into her and sent her flying.

Again.

He'd whispered the word so quietly against her mouth. His hands had already slid between them. She caught the rasp of a zipper, the tear of foil. The sounds might have been the most erotic she'd ever heard. Even as he sheathed himself, the need inside her had spiked into craving. She had to have him inside her. She couldn't survive another ten seconds if he wasn't.

Now. Right now.

He'd dug fingers into her hips, lifting her as she'd wrapped arms and legs around him. Then he'd driven into her, and she hadn't cared if she survived at all. His thrusts had battered her against the door again and again. Fast. As if he'd needed this to survive just as much as she had. That was the last rational thought she'd registered before his release triggered an orgasm that had simply shattered her.

Drawing in a deep breath, Cilla pressed a hand against her hammering heart. A little side-trip down memory lane was not going to help her find her panties. All it made her want to do was crawl back into bed with Jonah.

Don't think about that. No more fantasies, either. That's what had landed her in this situation—a one-night stand in a hotel near the Denver airport with Jonah Stone—a man she'd met for the first time only yesterday.

Her new job at G.W. Securities had brought her to a small family gathering at the Fortune Mansion in Denver. The moment she'd arrived at the party, she'd been aware of him. He was a man that any female would look at more than once—tall, dark and ruggedly handsome. He was dressed in a black turtleneck and jeans, which enhanced the broad shoulders, muscled chest and long, lanky legs. His chin was strong, his mouth firm and his cheekbones made her think of a warrior's.

Of course, she'd looked at him more than once or twice. Any woman needed a little eye candy in her life, right? It was when her eyes had finally collided with his that the trouble had started.

She'd heard that click, and she'd totally lost track of where she was, who she was. For seconds, minutes maybe, she hadn't been aware of anyone or anything but him. A stranger she'd seen across a crowded room.

It was the kind of thing she'd only read about in books or heard in song lyrics or seen in a movie. Everything had frozen, including time.

Before yesterday afternoon, Cilla would have sworn

that nothing like that could happen in real life. But it had. More astonishing than that, it had happened to her. And of course, she'd been curious.

Who was he?

And how could he have this amazing effect on her?

As a top-notch security agent and investigator, she'd tracked down the answer to her first question within five minutes. His name was Jonah Stone, and he was the best friend of her new boss, Gabe Wilder. That alone would pretty much have classified Mr. Tall, Dark and Handsome as forbidden fruit. The new G.W. Securities office in San Francisco was only six months old, and Gabe had hired her to run it. She *had* to concentrate on her job, on proving herself to Gabe. The last thing she needed was to get involved with his best friend.

But there was another reason to put Jonah Stone on the Forbidden Fruit list. From what Gabe had told her, his friend was a busy and successful entrepreneur, the owner of three successful supper clubs and totally focused on his businesses. That reminded her a bit too much of her father.

But even with the warning flags flying, she'd still tried to satisfy her curiosity about the second question. How could he have that time-stopping, nothing-else-matters effect on her mind and senses? So when he'd approached her, she'd gripped his outstretched hand, felt the hard palm, the firm strength of his fingers, and the oddest feeling of connection. Then she'd met his eyes and her mind had just emptied. And she'd been struck by a vivid image of the two of them, naked and rolling across a wide bed in a dark room.

Both the feeling and the image had faded, and she'd been just fine. But she'd also made her excuses and left the party early. And everything would have been fine if it hadn't been for the damn blizzard.

If the Denver airport hadn't had to close down last night, she and Jonah would have both been back in San Francisco in their separate apartments, and her expensive red panties would have been in her laundry hamper.

But it *had* shut down and she'd decided to switch to an early-morning flight and stay at the airport hotel. She'd been in the bar having a glass of wine and thinking about him when he'd shown up. During the time it had taken him to cross to her table and join her, she'd experienced for the third time in her life what she'd decided to call the nobody-else-but-Jonah effect.

For a moment, neither one of them had spoken. And then he'd made his proposition. And she'd agreed to it. The rest of the night was now history—and the sexiest one she'd ever experienced.

Panties, she reminded herself as she inched her way around the corner of the bed. *Find them. Get dressed. Leave.* The sooner she got back to San Francisco, the better.

They weren't anywhere along the foot of the bed. They weren't anywhere in the trail of clothes that led to the bed. Chances were good that they were still *in* the bed. But if she got back into that bed, it wouldn't be just for her expensive underwear.

She spotted the red lace the moment she crawled around the end of the bed to Jonah's side. In the light from the digital clock radio on the nightstand, she also saw Jonah. More of him than she wanted to. He was sprawled on his stomach, one arm dangling over the side of the mattress. The sheet covered him only to the waist.

And that strongly muscled back was not what she should be looking at. She dragged her gaze away and glanced down his arm to where his fingers nearly brushed the floor. Threaded through them was her quarry. All she had to do was get those panties and leave.

Very quietly, she crawled forward, scarcely daring to breathe. Gripping just the edge of the lace, she tugged.

Jonah's fingers reflexively clenched the red undies.

Cilla waited, listening hard. His breathing was steady. Only his fingers had moved, so in another moment, they'd relax again. This time she'd just pull harder.

That was one strategy—the smart one. Grab and go.

But her gaze had already betrayed her. It had left the panties behind to run up that arm. Jonah's face was turned toward her and his eyes, those incredible eyes, were closed.

She could easily wake him. There were a lot of ways to persuade a man to give up a piece of lace. Several scenarios ran through her mind.

She snuck a quick look at the clock: 5:15 a.m. The alarm hadn't yet sounded. Technically, it was still night. And if a girl only had one night to spend with a man?

She might as well make the most of it.

Rising, she pulled the sheet down and climbed back onto the bed to straddle Jonah. Then she leaned down to nibble at his ear and whisper, "I have a proposition for you."

2

Yet another sexy silent night, 2:00 a.m., three weeks later...

JONAH STONE STOOD AT the window of his apartment, looking out at his own private view of the Golden Gate Bridge. For almost a month now, he'd stood at the same place, delaying the time before he would inevitably have to climb up the stairs to his loft and go to bed. Once he did, he'd dream of her again.

Cilla Michaels.

The dreams that had been haunting him since the one night they'd spent together at that airport hotel in Denver were growing more vivid. In each of them, she'd be with him, right there in his bed. The sensations were always so intense. He'd smell that elusive scent of hers, feel her heart beat beneath his lips, taste the salty dampness of her skin under her breasts, the sweetness at her throat, her inner thighs, hear the way his name sounded when she gasped it into the silent night.

Steeped in her, he'd rise above her and look into

those incredibly green eyes as he entered her. Again and again, he'd thrust into her until he lost all of himself.

Then he'd wake to find himself alone in the bed. And he'd try to convince himself that was the way he wanted it.

One night. That's what he'd promised himself and her. That's what she'd agreed to. The memory of that night should have faded by now. That's what memories did. But everything about that night was still vividly etched in his mind.

Turning, Jonah glanced at the conference table where he'd left his cell phone. Next to it sat a small green box with a red ribbon. Cilla ran G.W. Securities' new office in San Francisco. So he could use the threatening note that had been tucked inside the box as a professional excuse to call her. Was that why he'd delayed calling his friend Gabe Wilder about it? So that he could call Cilla instead? He'd been tempted to do so more nights now than he could count. More than once he'd punched part of her number into his cell before he'd been able to stop himself.

The little green box with the red bow had been delivered to him that evening just when the cocktail hour at Pleasures had been its busiest. Since his apartment took up the third floor of the building, he frequently filled in for his manager, Virgil, on Monday nights.

He continued to study the box, debating. He'd been in the bar when his steady customer and current business partner, Carl Rockwell, had brought the small gift to him. Before he could thank him, Carl had explained that a man dressed up as Santa had given it to him just outside and asked him to deliver it.

Jonah had felt something the moment he'd taken the box, a tightening in his gut. The hairs on the back of his neck had stirred, too. He'd even turned to look through the windows that lined the wall of the bar to see if whoever had sent the gift might still be watching. There was no sign of a Santa.

Then he'd put the gift behind the bar and out of his mind as a new wave of customers streamed into the club. He hadn't opened it until a short time ago when he'd returned to his apartment. Moving to the table, he took the lid off the box and picked up the folded note he'd found inside.

'Tis the season for remembering Christmases past. Pleasures and fortune are fleeting. You destroyed an innocent life in pursuit of yours. You'll pay for that soon. Six nights and counting…

Rereading it had his gut instinct kicking in again. Perhaps it was the wording. And there was something else that kept tugging at the corners of his mind. Some memory that was eluding him. Maybe it was the reference to Christmases past. At twenty-nine he had a lot of them to remember and several that he'd tried hard to forget. Especially that long-ago one when his father had promised to return, but hadn't.

He'd also made his share of enemies. Some of them probably dated back to his early days in foster care. He hadn't always "played well with other children." As a businessman, he was demanding. He hired and fired people. Over the past six years he'd opened three successful supper clubs in the United States and he was in the process of opening another one in San Diego and a possible fifth in Rome.

Pleasures had been his first supper club and the result of a dream that had taken shape during his years in business school. His goal had been to create a place where people could escape into a different world and find temporary respite from the harsher realities of life. And he'd known that he wanted to open the club in San Francisco as a kind of thank-you to the saint the city had been named after, a saint who'd played an important part in his life.

The success of Pleasures had allowed him to open Interludes, a sports-themed bar in San Francisco, and more recently Passions, another supper club in Denver.

He didn't like it at all that the word *pleasures* was used in the note. But perhaps he was overreacting. It was December 19, a peak time for his businesses, and he wasn't getting much sleep, thanks to Cilla Michaels.

So he wasn't going to alarm Gabe yet. And calling Cilla, who was running Gabe's newly opened office in San Francisco, would be a mistake on so many levels.

He strode back to the window. Not that he could put all the blame on her. He'd known from the first instant he'd seen her at that party in the Fortune Mansion that she was different. That she'd be different for him. Gut instinct again.

His eyes had been drawn to her the moment she'd entered the room. No surprise there. Any man would have given her a second look. Her face had grabbed his attention first with its delicate features and stubborn chin. But he certainly hadn't missed the slender, almost lanky body and those long legs that the charcoal-gray slacks showcased. But it hadn't been just her looks that had pulled at him. She seemed to radiate an energy that tugged at him on a gut level.

Then there were those green eyes. The first time he'd looked into them, he'd felt as if he'd taken a punch right in the solar plexus. And when he'd clasped her hand in his, for a moment, he hadn't wanted to let it go.

The last thing he wanted or needed right now was to pursue a relationship with a woman who could have that effect on him. A woman like that could change your life.

During the past year, he'd seen his two best friends, Gabe Wilder and Nash Fortune, meet the women they'd decided to spend the rest of their lives with. Nash had already married his former high school sweetheart, Bianca Quinn, and Gabe was planning to marry FBI agent Nicola Guthrie on Valentine's Day.

He was happy for his friends, but Jonah liked his life just the way it was. Simple and uncomplicated. The right woman could change that. But on that night nearly a month ago in Denver, had he listened to what his mind was telling him? Had he heeded his gut instinct?

No.

Instead, he'd reverted to the reckless style of his youth when his name had been renowned in the family-court system. He'd followed Cilla Michaels when she'd left the party. He'd even watched her in the airport like a stalker until her flight was canceled. Then he'd followed her to the airport hotel and booked a room. Finally, he'd walked into the lounge, sat down at her table, and propositioned her for a one-night stand.

In the business world, Jonah Stone was never impulsive. He studied his options, planned various strategies. And he was even more careful in his private life and relationships. He'd been nine when his father had decided to desert his family, nine and a half when his mother had stepped in front of a bus rather than go on without the love of her life. He'd vowed never to be that vulnerable to anyone. Happy ever after didn't happen. The most one could hope for was a happy right now.

Instinct told him that Cilla Michaels could have the power to make him hope for the impossible. He turned back to the table and let his gaze rest on the green box with its festive red ribbon. His instinct was telling him something about that box, too, and he might not be overreacting.

Once again, he debated calling Cilla and hiring G.W. Securities. He had no doubt that his friend Gabe would recommend she handle the case. She was here in San Francisco. Gabe was in Denver. And at the party, Gabe had spent some time singing Cilla's praises to him. She'd been involved in a high-profile personal security case in L.A. and she'd saved a client from a crazed stalker. In Gabe's opinion, she had a rare combination of intelligence and excellent instincts.

But if he called her, he'd also have her in his bed again.

He pressed his hands against his eyes and rubbed. He didn't have to decide tonight. In the morning, he was flying to Denver to attend the annual Christmas party at the Denver Boys and Girls Club, a place he'd been running for years with Gabe and Nash. They'd opened the club when the St. Francis Center for Boys, the place where they'd all first met, had closed down. He'd discuss the box and the note with Gabe.

Jonah moved toward the spiral staircase to his loft. And there was always the chance that tonight would be the night that Cilla Michaels finally faded from his dreams.

CILLA JOLTED AWAKE AND TRIED to focus. Relief came when she realized she'd fallen asleep on the couch and not in her bed. During the past three weeks, she'd rationed the hours she allowed herself to spend in her bed.

Because the damn thing was cursed.

Each time she fell asleep in it she dreamed of Jonah Stone touching her, tormenting her, taking her.

And each time she woke up to find herself alone, she yearned for him. So avoiding her bed had become almost as important as avoiding Jonah.

Which was why she'd ended up dozing off on her couch during a Christmas movie marathon on the Hallmark Channel. The credits for *Miracle on 34th Street* were rolling down the screen. A quick glance at the time on her digital TV box confirmed that she'd dozed off for nearly twenty minutes.

That pissed her off.

Not only had she missed her favorite part of the movie, the part where Kris Kringle proves he really is Santa Claus, but she'd also missed the cheese and crackers. The plate sitting on the cushion beside her was now empty.

She glared at her cat. Flash, a plumply proportioned calico, lay stretched serenely along the arm of the sofa, a good distance from the scene of the crime.

Pets were not allowed at The Manderly Apartments, a rule that was explicitly spelled out in the lease and articulated equally clearly by the apartment manager, Mrs. Ortiz, a woman who reminded Cilla eerily of Mrs. Danvers in the old *Rebecca* movie.

But Flash hadn't given Cilla much choice. When she'd moved in a few months ago, the calico had migrated from its former home on the fire escape to the living room via an open window. And stayed.

It had to be for either the food or the conversation

since the cat wouldn't allow her to stroke, cuddle or even pick her up most of the time.

"You're supposed to share," Cilla pointed out.

Flash's bland expression clearly said, "You snooze, you lose."

Her phone rang and the caller ID lady chimed, "Call from Wilder, Gabe."

Cilla sprang from the sofa and raced for her desk. Gabe headed up G.W. Securities' home base in Denver. Two months ago he'd given her a new beginning by hiring her to manage his branch office in San Francisco when she'd moved on from a personal security agency in L.A. Gabe wouldn't be calling her at home on her night off if it wasn't important.

Maybe he even had a job for her. Business had been good lately. G.W. Securities offered a variety of services to corporate as well as private clients. Lots of people wanted to give security systems for Christmas, and she enjoyed the challenge of working on their design. But there were times when she missed the action that came with providing personal security.

Mentally crossing her fingers, she grabbed the receiver on the third ring. "Gabe."

"I hope I'm not interrupting anything important."

"Not at all." The cheese and crackers were gone, her favorite movie was over, and working would give her a perfect excuse to avoid her bed.

"I need a favor," Gabe said.

Cilla's heart sank. Not a job after all. "What can I do?"

"I want you to meet someone at the airport and make sure he gets home safely. He's not a client. He doesn't even know I'm making this phone call."

Hearing the worry in his voice, Cilla reached for a

pen and paper. "Who is he and what time does his plane touch down?"

On the other end of the line, Gabe expelled a breath. "Thanks, Cilla. It's Jonah Stone and he's due to arrive in San Francisco at 10:15. There was a lengthy delay because of the weather here in Denver. I was hoping the flight would be canceled, but he's on his way."

Jonah Stone.

Just the mention of his name had her heart skipping a beat. His image flashed into her mind—all that glorious dark hair, the handsome face with its sharp cheekbones, clearly defined chin with just that hint of a cleft, and the dark gray eyes... Just thinking about him made her knees weak and she carefully lowered herself into her desk chair.

"Jonah's not going to like that I'm sending you," Gabe said.

Cilla didn't imagine that he would. She'd had a chance to explore every inch of that taut, toned, amazing body. Jonah was a man who could handle himself on a physical level pretty well. That was definitely part of what made him so damned attractive.

More than once since their night in Denver, she'd regretted the fact that he was on her Forbidden Fruit list. More than once, she'd run over the reasons why. She'd done a little research on him. According to Gabe, the man had a real talent for hacking and electronic security, and right out of college, he'd helped Gabe establish G.W. Securities and continued to work there while he'd recruited backers for a supper club in San Francisco. In the past six years, he'd opened two more clubs and others were in the planning stages. A man that successful had to put business first just as her father had.

And still did. Bradley Michaels was handsome,

charming and currently working as the CEO of his fourth company. There'd been no time in his life for her mother or her. Not even at Christmas. Christmas had been his time to focus even more on the business and entertaining. After five years of playing second fiddle, her mother had divorced him, and since then Cilla's contact with her father had been limited to phone calls on her birthday and Christmas.

"I'm worried about Jonah," Gabe said.

"Why?"

"Because *he's* worried enough to cancel his plans and fly back to San Francisco early. He received a threatening note today. It was inside a green box tied with red ribbon and hand delivered to him while he was at a Christmas party he and Father Mike Flynn and I were throwing for the Boys and Girls Club we run here in Denver. I have some people still working on the box and the ribbon, but there were no prints, and I've had no luck tracking down the sender. He or she wore a Santa suit and sent it in with one of the kids. An early present for Mr. Stone. I'll send the contents of the note right now in a text."

Cilla grabbed her cell phone. "It's the first one he's received?"

"No. I asked him that right away and he admitted getting one yesterday during the height of the cocktail hour at Pleasures."

"I've got the text." Then she read it aloud.

""'Tis the season for remembering Christmases past. Pleasures and fortune are fleeting. You destroyed an innocent life in pursuit of yours. You'll pay for that soon. Five nights and counting...'"

Today was the twentieth of December. Cilla did the math in her head. "Five nights until Christmas."

"Yeah. The first had the exact same message except that it read, 'Six nights and counting…'"

Holding the phone pressed to her ear, Cilla rose and began to pace. "The first one is delivered to his club here in San Francisco, the next to Denver. The sender wants him to know that someone's keeping close tabs on him."

"We think along the same lines, and so does Jonah."

"Does anything in the wording ring a bell for him?" Cilla asked.

"Not that he can put a finger on. But he has a feeling about the threat. His feelings are usually spot-on, so now I have one, too."

She was beginning to get one herself. Gut instinct should never be ignored. Her mind was already racing ahead. What she had was a reluctant client and the possibility of real danger. A tricky combination, but she could do tricky. In fact, she enjoyed tricky. One reason she'd been delighted when Gabe had approached her was because the jobs in L.A. had become a bit too predictable and boring even before she'd had a disagreement with a client and decided to move on.

"Jonah has an office and living quarters over his club, Pleasures. That's where he's headed."

"Good to know." Going to Pleasures would mean a wardrobe change. The jeans she was wearing would be out of place at the fancy supper club.

"I've known Jonah since we were in our teens. Ask him for help and he'll give you anything he's got. But at heart, he's a bit of a loner. He doesn't like to depend on anyone."

"In other words, he's going to try to ditch me."

"Yeah. He wouldn't let me send anyone with him. He wouldn't even let me tag along."

"Don't worry. I'll stick." The two years she'd spent working personal security for some of Hollywood's youngest and brattiest stars had honed her skills in the sticking department.

The moment she hung up the phone, she raced into her bedroom and threw open her closet door. She didn't have a lot of clothes, but during her time in L.A., she'd acquired some special pieces. She pushed aside hangars and decided on the little black cocktail dress that had visited some of Hollywood's hottest nightspots.

Whirling, she was about to toss it onto her bed, but Flash lay sprawled across the middle. The cat could move like lightning when she really wanted to.

"I have to leave for a while." She tried to keep the excitement out of her voice. "Business. Fancy place."

Pleasures was very upscale. Though she'd never been there, she'd frequently walked by. And each time she'd passed the front doors during the past three weeks, she'd resisted the temptation to go in. If she had, the chances were good that she'd run into him. The plan was to get over Jonah Stone.

So far the plan hadn't worked. And seeing him again…

Jonah was a client, she reminded herself. And she had very strict rules about clients.

She turned her attention to Flash. "Dress needs something, don't you think?" The red peep-toed shoes had cost her half a paycheck, but when she held them up for Flash's inspection, the cat made a sound deep in her throat.

"I agree. These things will dress up anything."

It took her three minutes to change and another ten before she was satisfied with her hair and makeup.

She paused to survey herself in the mirror. She definitely didn't look like a bodyguard. That ought to make it easier for a man like Jonah Stone to accept her as one. At least for the evening.

Then she narrowed her eyes on the image in the mirror and swept her gaze down and up. "Who are you kidding? You're wearing this just as much for him as you are for the job."

Moving closer, she tapped a finger on the mirror. "The man has three strikes against him. Not only is he like your father, he's also your boss's best friend and now he's a client. One night with Jonah Stone is understandable. Enviable. Any more could be disastrous. You are going to handle this."

Turning back to her closet, she grabbed her red leather coat and transferred her gun from her dresser drawer to her pocket. She was almost at the door of her apartment before she felt the eyes boring into her back.

Flash.

"Sorry." Whipping around, she saw that the cat had returned to her station on the sofa. Right next to the empty plate.

"I've got to go, pal." Crossing to the sofa, she crouched down and looked into Flash's eyes. "It shouldn't take long. But it's my chance to impress my new boss." She lifted a hand and then dropped it, reminding herself that Flash didn't like to be touched. "No more food. Remember our little talk about lifestyle choices."

It was one that they'd had several times since she'd taken her new roommate to the vet. Dr. Robillard had prescribed a "modification" in Flash's diet. The pediatrician her mother had taken Cilla to when she was thirteen had used nearly the same words.

"Moderation is the key. It made all the difference for me when I was in my teens. You'll get used to it."

Flash's expression said, "You've got to be kidding."

"Tell you what. I'll leave the Hallmark Channel on. They're having a marathon of Christmas movies. It'll take your mind off food." She snagged the remote, hit the channel. "Look. *A Boyfriend for Christmas.* That sounds like a great one. Santa, presents and romance thrown in."

And now she didn't have to watch it herself. Cilla silently sent up a prayer of thanksgiving to Gabe as she rose and raced for the door.

"Meeow."

Flash's mournful reproach followed Cilla as she headed for the stairs.

3

Jonah Stone hadn't been having the best of days when he stepped into the airport parking garage. A chilly blast of wind followed him. His flight to San Francisco had been delayed three hours because of a blizzard in Denver, and he'd spent most of his wait time at the airport thinking about another blizzard and another night.

He'd been counting on the time in Denver to give him some respite from thoughts of Cilla. He'd been looking forward to catching up with his best friend, Gabe Wilder. Their other pal Nash hadn't been able to make their annual party because his grandmother had arranged for a private Christmas cruise that would allow Nash and his wife, Bianca, to get to know some recently discovered members of their family.

Though their career paths had drawn them apart since the years they'd spent at Denver's St. Francis Center for Boys, they tried to get together whenever they could, and Christmas usually provided the perfect time. He'd been looking forward to a poker game tonight at Gabe's apartment and shooting some hoops tomorrow.

The note that had been hand delivered that morning

had changed his plans. Like the first, it had come in a small green box tied with a red ribbon. The message had been playing in his head in a continuous loop, and each time it repeated, the feeling in his gut grew stronger.

The word *pleasures* had appeared in both notes, so now he was headed back to the club. Pulling his parking stub out of his pocket, he checked the aisle, turned left, and increased his pace.

He nearly stopped dead in his tracks when he saw her. Though he managed not to break stride, he now knew what it must be like to take two barrels of a shotgun right in the belly. She was leaning against the back fender of his car, her mile-long legs crossed in front of her.

Cilla Michaels.

As often as he'd considered calling her, as frequently as he'd imagined her in his mind, nothing had prepared him for the impact that seeing her again would have on him.

It was all he could do to keep his pace from quickening. That night in the hotel lounge, her dark hair had been pulled back into a long neat braid. Tonight, it spilled in dark curls over her shoulders. The open red leather trench coat revealed a very short black dress. The shoes were red with open toes and dangerously high heels. And the legs…well, they were incredible.

But as he reached her, it was the eyes that drew his gaze again, just as they had before. They were a pure and piercing green with a shimmer of gold around the pupils. Fascinating. And looking into them for too long had the same effect he'd experienced the first time. He forgot to breathe.

When he drew air in, he felt the burn in his lungs.

No other woman had ever affected his senses, his mind, his breathing, his gut in quite this way.

Nearly a month had passed and he hadn't stopped wanting her. Now, seeing her again, he wanted her even more. He wanted his hands on her. He needed hers on him.

All the more reason to remember that she was dangerous for him. All the more reason to send her away. He had bigger problems on his plate right now. The two notes he'd received needed all of his attention.

"Cilla Michaels," he said. "Gabe sent you."

She nodded. "He contacted me as soon as your plane left Denver. He thinks you need protection, and he warned me you might not like it."

"It's not a matter of liking. Do I look like someone who needs protection?"

"Not in the least." Cilla had had plenty of time to study him as he'd walked toward her, but she was sorely tempted to run her gaze over him again. The black leather jacket and jeans suited his tall, lanky frame and made him look tough and a little dangerous.

"You look to me as if you could handle yourself just fine," she said.

"Good." He opened the passenger door and tossed his duffel on the seat. "Then we're agreed that I don't need your services."

"We're not agreed on that." She waited until he met her eyes, then added, "The least you can do is let me give my sales pitch. It's the job of G.W. Securities to think of things the client might overlook."

He leaned a hip against the car door. "Such as?"

"Would you have thought to check for a bomb under your car?"

He narrowed his gaze. "No."

She smiled. "I did. It's part of the service." She could tell from the look in his eyes that she might have scored a point, but the game wasn't over.

"I know that the first note said, 'six days and counting…'" she continued, "the second said five, but that could be a lie. Sociopaths aren't known for their honesty."

Silence.

"And you're probably thinking it's highly unlikely that someone could have traced your car to this particular parking space, but I got a friend of mine to run down your license plate. Then I simply drove through the garage until I located your car. If I was able to do that, so could someone else. They could easily have booby-trapped it."

"Okay, you've made your point." When he smiled at her, the effect rippled right down to her toes. Then he took the lapel of her jacket and rubbed it between his fingers. Her toes, the little traitors, curled.

"But you've obviously got better things to do tonight. From the looks of it, Gabe's call pulled you away from something or someone special."

She thought of the empty cheese and cracker plate, her disgruntled cat and the movie on the Hallmark Channel's Countdown to Christmas and barely smothered a yawn. Instead, she tried a smile of her own. "Actually, it didn't. I was having a quiet evening at home."

His eyebrow quirked up. "You dress like this for a quiet evening at home?"

"I changed after Gabe called. I thought this was more appropriate for Pleasures. That is where you're headed, isn't it?"

His smile faded. "Gabe is overreacting."

"He said you had a feeling."

"I may be overreacting. It's probably a crank."

"Perhaps." But in the three hours he'd sat in the Denver airport waiting for his plane, he hadn't changed his mind about coming home, Cilla thought. "But you don't think so. You don't like the fact that they used the word *pleasures* in the note."

Surprise flickered for a moment in his eyes. "No, I don't like that."

"Could be coincidence, but…"

"I don't trust coincidence."

"But you do trust your instincts."

He let the silence stretch again, so she pushed her advantage. "Look, I know we have a history. And we made a deal. One night." She waved a hand. "Let's put all of that in a side bar for now. This is strictly a professional offer."

He narrowed his eyes fractionally, and dammit, her toes curled again. For an instant, her mind flashed back to that moment in Denver when they'd first stepped into the hotel room and he'd pushed the door shut and put his hands on her. His eyes had narrowed then, too, and she recalled how they'd glinted in the darkness. Ignoring both the image and her traitorous toes, she ruthlessly focused.

"Gabe's a friend of yours and he's my boss. He asked me to make sure you got to Pleasures safely. As a favor. I'm not even here on G.W. Securities' clock. But I am here as a private security agent. And I'm good at what I do. You can call Gabe and get a recommendation."

He frowned. "I'm not questioning your abilities."

"Then why don't you think of my escorting you to your club as a way to set Gabe's mind at ease?"

"You'll follow me to Pleasures and that's it."

"Not exactly. The service G.W. Securities provides

is more than door-to-door. I check out your apartment before you go in. Double-check the security system. And I get a chance to walk you through Pleasures on the way. I've never been there."

He considered for a moment. "Sounds reasonable. I run the risk of sounding like a real prick if I say no."

"Not exactly the way I'd phrase it, but you've got the gist."

"You *are* good at this, aren't you?"

She beamed a smile at him. "I'm the best. How about I follow you to your club?"

HE LIKED TO KEEP HIS ROOM dark. In his opinion, everything was way too bright during the holiday season, as evidenced by the amount of light pouring through the windows. On the screen of his laptop, he could see that Jonah Stone's plane had landed—10:15.

The anger that he'd been keeping tightly leashed for the past three hours eased just a little. He didn't like it at all when he had to adjust his plans. The plane should have landed three hours ago.

But Stone was finally here. It wasn't too late to go forward with the scheme. It would be another forty-five minutes to an hour before Jonah Stone would reach Pleasures.

He took a cell phone from his desk and punched in a number. On the fourth ring, a raspy voice said, "Yeah?"

He relayed the information and gave the order. "Got that?"

"Consider it done."

Turning off the cell, he laid it carefully on the desk. Then he rose, walked to the closet and took out his overcoat, a hat and a long scarf. He trusted the man in charge of the mission, but he would still be on the scene to make sure his orders were carried out.

Five more nights—that's how long it would take to complete his mission. It was all planned out. And during those nights, Jonah Stone would pay for the life he'd taken.

Moving to the nightstand, he glanced down at the picture. It was framed in crystal, and a small flameless candle burned in front of it.

Elizabeth. Poor, innocent Elizabeth. She'd been the only person he'd ever loved. And he'd had to leave her. He had a calling. She'd understood. He'd known that she'd been fragile, but how could he have foreseen that in his absence, she would fall under the spell of a man who'd seduce her and then reject her and kill her?

Five nights from now, on the anniversary of her death, he would exact revenge.

After running one finger down the side of the frame, he put on his coat, the hat and the scarf. Then he walked to the door.

When one set up a plan, part of the pleasure was watching it come flawlessly to fruition.

4

"YOU'VE GOT A CLASSY PLACE here," Cilla remarked as she joined Jonah at the rear of his car. He'd pulled into a private lot half a block down from Pleasures and spoken briefly with the attendant, who'd then waved her through.

"I like it," he said, shifting his gaze to the three-story club on the corner across the street.

And well he should, Cilla decided as she studied it. The location was prime, right in the heart of the city, and the building was old with tall arched windows on two upper floors that recalled a different, more gilded age.

On the second floor, shadowy figures wove their way among tables lit with candles. Through the windows on the street level, she caught a glimpse of a crowded bar. Tiny white Christmas lights twinkled on the awning, a subtle salute to the season.

"I know that I only talked you into letting me escort you here and lock you up tight for the night, but you really should allow G.W. Securities to provide you with round-the-clock protection. At least until we get a handle on what's going on here."

"You talked to Gabe on the drive over."

She shrugged. "He is my boss. He wants to put a couple of men on you even without your agreement. My feeling is that the moment you spot them, you'll shake them. He agreed. So we'd like your permission."

"You've got all you're going to get from me tonight. I have a business meeting tomorrow afternoon, and I don't need a couple of babysitters tagging along. You can tell Gabe that I'll check for car bombs myself in the morning."

She let it rest as they watched a couple exit through the glossy red entrance doors to the club and head up the street in the opposite direction. At this time of night, there were very few pedestrians, and many of the other buildings on the block were dark. So were parked cars. In contrast, Pleasures glowed like a tempting little jewel.

"Shall we go clubbing?" he asked.

"Can't wait."

Jonah extracted his duffel from the front seat and started across the lot. Behind them, the car beeped as he locked it with the remote.

She walked to his left, just half a step in front of him, and when they reached the sidewalk her eyes scanned the street. Directly across from them was a narrow alleyway, but the light from a streetlamp revealed only Dumpsters. To the left was an unmarked van in a loading zone. But it was seemingly empty and already sported a parking ticket on the windshield.

There was nothing at all to cause the itchy feeling at the back of her neck. The door of the club opened, releasing another couple along with the faint sound of bluesy music and laughter. The man and woman turned away from them, crossed to the opposite corner, then disappeared down a side street.

As they stepped off the sidewalk, Cilla slipped an arm through Jonah's, and drew him on an angle toward Pleasures. "I can't tell you how many times I've been tempted to drop in your club for just a drink."

He shot her a sideways glance. "Why haven't you?"

"Usually I'm not dressed for the occasion." That was true enough, but not the only reason she'd avoided going into the bar. "My apartment's not far from here, so I've walked by on my way home from work. You painted the doors red a few weeks ago."

"My manager Virgil's idea. He wanted to try it out for Christmas."

"Festive. One of these days I'll dress up and treat myself to a glass of champagne at the bar."

"We don't have a dress code."

"But with a club like Pleasures, dressing up is part of the deal—kind of like Cinderella going to the ball. It wouldn't have been the same if she'd worn her work clothes to the castle. Know what I mean?"

"Yes." He looked over at the bright lights of the club. "I know exactly what you mean. Providing the opportunity to dress up and escape the workaday world is part of what each of my venues offers."

The itchy feeling that had been nagging her since they'd stepped out of the parking lot suddenly increased, and Cilla had to exert all her control not to turn around. Instead, she listened hard.

Some kind of movement near the van? Their backs were to it now. Then she heard the footsteps, approaching from behind.

When Jonah tensed beside her and would have turned, she increased the pressure on his arm and pitched her voice low. "We have company, so do exactly as I say. Take me into your arms."

She moved with him, shifting so that her body shielded his, then raised her hands to his face. "Lean closer."

He leaned so close that his lips were nearly brushing hers. She was very aware of the fact that the footsteps were growing louder. But she was aware of other things, too—a flood of sensations. The hardness of his body, the heat of his breath on her mouth, the ribbon of pleasure that unwound right to her toes. Every cell in her body remembered him. Wanted him. For a fleeting moment, one desire—to feel those lips on hers—nearly swamped her.

Ruthlessly refocusing, she whispered, "Be my eyes. How many, what do they look like, and how close are they?"

"Two and they look like Laurel and Hardy." He nipped at her bottom lip, and for just an instant, her mind clouded, then emptied as if someone had pulled a plug. She was aware only of Jonah—the hardness of his thighs against hers, the tightening of his hands at her waist, the heat of his breath as it moved over her lips and between them. Sensations hammered at her, and all she wanted was to melt into him.

"They're about ten feet away. And the fat one, Hardy, has a gun."

"Shit." Adrenaline spiked through her system, clearing her thoughts, stiffening her spine. "I need them closer."

"You're getting your wish, sugar."

"The one with the gun is mine."

"Not going to happen."

She nipped his bottom lip hard. "I know what I'm

doing. Here's how it's going to go down. I'll be the help-less female, you the macho man. He won't know what hit him. Trust me."

"Let the girl go," a gravelly voice said.

Arguing time was up, but Jonah dropped his hands. Cilla immediately pivoted toward the men. Eyes widen-ing, she pressed a hand against her breast and focused on her training. "Sweetums, he's got a gun."

"Step aside," the tall, skinny one said to her. "We don't want you."

"Go ahead, sugar," Jonah said. "Run on up to the club. I can handle this."

"Okay. Okay." The words came out on breathless gasps as she took one shaky step, sideways. Without missing a beat, she shot her other leg straight up. Her toe hit Fatso's wrist dead-on and the gun clattered to the pavement. Pivoting slightly, she landed a punch to the man's temple. With a grunt, Fatso fell like a rock.

She glanced up to see Jonah racing after the skinny one. "Dammit!"

Pausing only long enough to kick the gun on the sidewalk out of the way, she ran after them. Her heart shot straight to her throat when the back door of the van near the alley slid open. There was at least one more thug to deal with—the driver. She could see him through the windshield now. Broad shoulders, short gray hair.

Before skinny could nose-dive through the door, Jonah grabbed him by the collar and spun him around. One punch straight to the face took him down. Cilla winced and for the first time registered the sting in her own knuckles.

Then the window on the driver's side lowered and she saw the gun.

"Get down," she shouted to Jonah. He did, hitting the sidewalk and rolling as the shot rang out. Skidding to a stop, she pulled her own gun out of her pocket, gripping it in both hands as she took her stance and fired. Tires squealing, the van lurched away from the curb and up the street. It backfired loudly in the intersection, then roared off. She got the license plate before it disappeared.

Sliding her weapon back in her pocket, she turned to see that Jonah had already sprung to his feet. The relief was so intense that for a moment she couldn't speak. Then she said, "I told you to trust me. I said I could handle it. You could have gotten yourself shot."

So could she, Jonah thought as he walked toward her. He'd rolled over quickly enough to see that she hadn't dropped to the ground as she'd told him to do. Instead, she'd stood there, feet spread, returning the fire of the man in the van like some mythical warrior. He was certain that his heart had skipped two whole beats.

"From my perspective, you did handle it. Very well. I'm not shot, and Laurel and Hardy are out for the count."

He'd taken her arm to draw her with him toward the club. It was only then that he saw they'd attracted an audience. From the looks of it, most of the bar crowd had poured into the street including Virgil, the tall, bronze-skinned man who'd managed Pleasures since Jonah had opened it.

The fat guy he'd nicknamed Hardy was on his hands and knees, shaking his head like a dog. When they reached him, Cilla planted one of her shoes right under his nose where he could see it. "Don't even think of getting up unless you want me to kick you again."

He collapsed onto his stomach.

"Boss," Virgil said. "You all right?"

"Fine. You'd better call the police. Ms. Michaels and I seem to have been the victims of an attempted mugging."

"I already called 9-1-1, and so did several of our customers."

Even as sirens sounded in the distance, Jonah noted that Cilla had crouched down to secure the fat guy's hands behind his back. When she'd finished, there was a spattering of applause from the people who'd gathered. Ignoring it, she retrieved the first man's gun, then secured the man Jonah had knocked out.

Jonah turned to Virgil. "If you wouldn't mind, could you stay here and keep everyone away from the crime scene until the police arrive?"

Jonah saw the questions in his manager's eyes. He also read concern, but all Virgil said was, "Sure thing, but I don't think these guys are going anywhere."

"No." He glanced back as Cilla walked toward him. The sound of sirens grew closer. "I'll try to reassure our guests. You can send the police to me when they arrive."

When Cilla reached him, she put her arm through his and kissed him on the cheek. "You sure know how to show a girl an exciting time." Then she turned to beam a smile at the small crowd of onlookers. "I'm pretty lucky."

There was more murmuring and nods of agreement. One woman said, "I think he's the lucky one. The only other place I've seen a kick like that was when I saw the Rockettes at Radio City Music Hall."

There were more nods and a few laughs as his customers began to move back into the club.

"I'm going to offer everyone a round of free drinks,

but you've already diminished the tension level considerably," he murmured as they followed the group.

"You can thank me by trusting me more the next time," she hissed.

Jonah laughed as he drew her into Pleasures.

AN HOUR LATER, JONAH sat in his office watching Cilla pace back and forth in front of his desk, talking on the phone to Gabe. Making her report.

The policemen had questioned them separately, and the one who was in charge, Detective Finelli, seemed to know Cilla. Which reminded Jonah very forcibly that he knew very little about her—only what Gabe had told him at the party. Her name was Priscilla Michaels, but she went by Cilla, and Gabe thought the world of her.

Oh, he'd been tempted to run a thorough background check on her, but satisfying curiosity could lead a man into deep trouble. Finding out more about her could have complicated his decision to keep his distance.

The name Priscilla intrigued him because it didn't fit the woman he'd spent the night with in Denver. Cilla suited her better. It also fit the woman he'd met at the airport and the one who'd turned into his arms out on the street. For an instant when she'd put her hands on his face and pulled his head down to hers, he could have sworn the cement beneath his feet had shifted as if it were beach sand. And all he'd been able to think of was her.

Oh, she was a very dangerous woman. And like it or not, he was learning more about her with each moment that passed. Problem was, the more he discovered, the more curious and fascinated he became. She was good at what she did. She'd not only smoothly maneuvered him earlier into accepting her escort back to Pleasures, but once the police had left, she'd managed to get a call into Gabe before he had.

And the woman who paced in front of him right now was a sharp right turn from the woman who'd met him at the airport earlier or the woman who'd kicked the gun out of that thug's hand. Ever since she'd entered Pleasures, it was as if she'd had a to-do list and she'd been checking off items one by one. Quick, efficient, focused.

It occurred to him that he was dealing with two sides of the same woman. He recalled his first reaction to her given name. But Priscilla fit the woman he was watching now to a T.

She paused in her pacing to fist a hand on her hip and summarize for Gabe what Detective Finelli had assured them before he'd left. The police would do everything they could do—question Fatso and Skinny, put out an all-points bulletin on the van.

"The two men have lawyered up, so they won't be questioned until the morning when their public defenders are assigned," Cilla said to Gabe as she started to pace again. "But my friend Joe Finelli says he'll talk to his captain and get permission for me to observe the interviews."

Her friend Joe Finelli? Jonah recalled what he'd seen of the interaction between the detective and Cilla. Finelli was a good ten years her senior. Had they dated? Been lovers?

And the fact that his mind instantly jumped to those questions reminded him why he'd decided to avoid Cilla Michaels. He didn't want that kind of involvement.

Deliberately he looked past her to the open door of his office. The evening was winding down. By the time the police cars had pulled away, he could see that everything had returned to normal in his club. The bar was still busy, and the jazz band on the basement level would switch to dance music in another half hour.

Virgil would handle closing. What Jonah needed was some quiet time in his apartment to try to figure out what in hell was going on. There was something in the wording of the note that was still pulling at the edge of his mind.

"Joe recommended that he continue with private security," Cilla was saying.

Joe. Her use of the detective's first name triggered a quick surge of impatience. Not jealousy. Because that was ridiculous. And the impatience was with himself.

Because he didn't want to go to his apartment and think about what had happened by himself. He wanted to talk about it with Cilla Michaels. And perhaps with Priscilla, too.

He watched her stride across the width of his office again and wondered if the woman ever stood still. There was such energy radiating off her. She'd been lightning fast outside the club—both physically and mentally. The kick had come out of nowhere. The poor sucker hadn't been expecting it.

And she'd brought those same elements of energy and surprise to her lovemaking, as well. He vividly recalled the speed of those clever hands as they'd moved over his skin exploring, exploiting—until the flood of razor-sharp sensations had left him helpless to do anything but want more.

"Sure I can set up a security detail." Cilla paused at his desk to pull a small notebook and pen out of her purse. "We'll want to give him 24/7 protection, two men each shift."

Jonah took a deep breath and brought his focus back

to her. He wasn't helpless. This time it was more than a surge of impatience he felt. Sitting on the sidelines and letting others decide his fate had never been his strong suit. He'd run away from three foster homes before the judge tired of seeing his face and sent him to Father Mike at the St. Francis Center for Boys.

At the time Father Mike had a reputation in the Denver area for being able to handle "bad" or "problem" boys. Jonah figured he'd been both. And if it hadn't been for the center and the fact that he'd met Nash and Gabe there, he wouldn't be where he was today.

"I'll handle it," Cilla said.

Studying her, Jonah leaned back in his chair. He was used to handling his own affairs or handpicking the people he chose to delegate them to. And whenever he could, he chose people he knew and trusted. Virgil had been like a big brother to him in the first foster home he was sent to. Before he'd opened Pleasures, he'd tracked Virgil down and hired him to manage the club. When he'd opened his sports bar, Interludes, he'd offered the manager's position to Carmen D'Annunzio, a woman who'd volunteered at the St. Francis Center when her boys were in their early teens.

But he hadn't chosen Cilla Michaels. He'd decided not to choose her, hadn't he? She sat on the edge of his desk, her cell phone tucked beneath her ear as she scribbled. "I think we can cover it for now."

We meaning who? He definitely didn't like hearing the plans being made as if he were…what? A client whose life she'd just saved?

Jonah frowned. That was exactly the case, wasn't it? If Cilla Michaels hadn't met him at the airport and pressured him into accepting her escort, he might very well be lying on the sidewalk outside just as Laurel and Hardy had been doing when the police arrived. In fact, he might have a bullet hole in him.

His frown deepened. That scenario didn't jibe with the note that had been delivered to him. If someone wanted to gun him down on the street, why warn him about it first? And why bother counting down the nights until Christmas? Unless the two incidents weren't connected.

That was something he wanted to talk to her about. Priscilla would have a theory. He was sure of it.

And then there was Cilla.

She strode away from his desk and put her hand on her hip again. The red coat was shoved back, giving him a good view of those remarkable legs. And he remembered exactly how it had felt when they'd been wrapped around him.

It could happen again. Something primal, something that went beyond desire, sparked to life inside of him. In seconds, he could move to the door, lock it and take her against it just as he had in that hotel room in Denver. Seconds and he could have his mouth on hers. God, he wanted that. He wanted to taste her again— that sweet, tart flavor that grew more complex each time he feasted on it. He wanted to touch her again, to push the hem of that dress up those long, silky legs. Seconds. It would take only seconds to sheath himself and push aside whatever lacy barrier was left between them. Then he would fill her. She would surround him.

The image in his mind triggered sensations so vivid that he could almost feel her closing around him as he thrust into her. Seconds, he thought again. Seconds and he could turn the fantasy in his mind into reality. The temptation to do just that was so powerful, Jonah had to grip the arms of the chair tight.

This was why he'd stayed away for nearly a month, he reminded himself. And this was why he should keep his distance now.

"No, we haven't talked about it yet, but I'm sure he'll agree that private security is the way to go," Cilla said. When she shot him a questioning look, Jonah merely returned a bland one.

He wasn't a fool. Until he could figure out what was going on, he was going to take precautions. A bodyguard wouldn't be a bad idea.

"I can free up David Santos and Mark Gibbons," Cilla said. "They're very good, and I can still handle our other clients."

Jonah refocused his attention on what she was saying.

She slid him a sideways glance. "Great. I'll let him know."

Let him know? Annoyance sizzled through him. Mostly at himself. All evening, he'd let her call the shots. She'd convinced him to let her follow him to Pleasures, then she'd maneuvered him into that little macho man/poor helpless female scenario when the two thugs had approached. And she'd been the one who'd reported everything to Gabe. Now if he'd heard right, she intended to step back and assign two other men to guard him.

That wasn't her decision to make. He was about to stretch out his hand and demand to talk to Gabe when she closed her cell and faced him across the desk.

"We need to talk," she said.

"Indeed we do." Jonah kept his gaze on Cilla for one

long moment before he rose and said, "Before you tell me what you and Gabe have decided, let me introduce you to Pleasures."

5

HE WALKED FOR OVER AN HOUR in an attempt to settle his rage. The wind blowing in from the Bay carried a fine, icy mist that stung his cheeks. In spite of the cold and the lateness of the hour, there were still some people walking along the Embarcadero, wandering to and from Fisherman's Wharf.

Normally, he would have avoided the lights and the seasonal decorations, but tonight he would use them as reminders.

Of Elizabeth.

Of his loss.

Of his mission.

But in spite of the litany that he repeated in his mind, every time he thought of what had happened at Pleasures, his fury threatened to rise up like a tidal wave and consume him. At times, the red haze in front of his eyes nearly blinded him.

His plan, his perfect plan had been bungled! Even now, as he replayed the scene in his mind, the panic and anger bubbled up just as it had when he'd been parked down the street from the club.

He'd wanted to jump out of his car and scream.

But he'd controlled the urge. Even when he'd heard the gunshots, he hadn't allowed the panic to take control. His first impulse had been to follow the van and confront his partner. But acting when he was still teetering on the brink of anger would have been a mistake.

Instead, he'd made himself wait until the crowd had gone back into Pleasures, then he'd pulled out of his space and driven down to Fisherman's Wharf.

Just a little bit longer now, and he'd be fine. Something inside of him would settle and his mind would clear.

For two blocks, he concentrated on breathing in and breathing out. No one had seen him earlier. He was sure of that. Everyone had been watching what was going on in front of the club. But he shouldn't have panicked.

That was inexcusable. Panic led to mistakes even when the anger was justified.

He'd explained the plan very carefully to his partner. It was a simple job.

No guns.

Fury erupted again. If they'd shot Jonah…

He bit back the scream that burned in his throat like acid and fisted his hands at his sides. It was *his* job to kill Jonah. His job. And it wasn't time yet.

When the red haze threatened to blur his vision again, he stopped and drew in a deep breath. Then another.

Think. He had to think.

It wasn't entirely his partner's fault that the mission had failed. There was the woman.

She shouldn't have been there. Jonah Stone wasn't dating anyone. She didn't work for him. And she'd spoiled everything.

He began to walk again. He'd find out who she was, and she'd pay dearly for disrupting his plan.

When he finally felt himself settle, he realized that he was standing in front of a restaurant. Through the windows, he saw people laughing and talking at the bar. For a moment, he was tempted to go in and order a drink. Then the door of the restaurant opened and he caught the sound of muted Christmas music.

No. He couldn't go into a place where they were celebrating the season.

So he would return to his room to have that drink, and he would wait for his partner to report.

And he would plan his revenge on the woman.

As JONAH LED HER AROUND on a brief tour of Pleasures, Cilla could tell he was seriously annoyed. The calm voice and the charming smile didn't fool her.

She could understand what he must be feeling, sympathize with it. But what she admired was the way he kept his emotions tightly leashed. He'd never once interrupted her or tried to take her cell phone from her while she was reporting to Gabe. She doubted she could have been that patient.

He'd taken her on a brief tour of the jazz room in the basement and the private dining rooms on the second floor, but she couldn't recall one detail. Each time his arm brushed against hers or he placed a hand on the small of her back to guide her up or down a staircase, she couldn't help remembering that moment out on the street when he'd leaned closer, his lips nearly brushing hers, and the incredible heat that had exploded through her.

For that one instant, her mind had totally blanked. She'd forgotten her plan, the danger he was in. There'd been only Jonah Stone. And the fierce desire that he alone could provoke had nearly consumed her.

He'd felt at least some of what she was feeling. His hands had tightened their grip on her waist and she'd seen the way those smoke-colored eyes had darkened until they were black as an abyss.

But he hadn't kissed her. He'd maintained control. He'd kept his mind focused on the danger. What woman could resist thinking about what it might take to break that control?

Which was reason numero uno why she had to take herself off the case. Jonah Stone was in trouble. And the best way she could help him was to keep her distance. So she could think—about something besides jumping him.

That last option was totally off the plate since he was now officially a client. In her book, getting involved with a client led to disaster. It was a client in L.A. who'd expected side benefits as part of his security service that had led her to quit and move on.

But Jonah Stone was an entirely different problem. This time she was the one who might be tempted to offer side benefits. Even now she could feel the slow burning flame that she'd felt from the first time he'd gripped her hand at Gabe's party. And she'd experienced how that flame could explode into a flash fire. Her aunt Nancy, who was a Catholic nun, used to talk about avoiding the occasion of sin. Cilla shot Jonah a sideways glance. For her that term summed up Jonah Stone.

And he was still in perfect control. There was no sign of what he had to be feeling. The man had gone through a lot today. Still, when they reached the bar, he smiled and exchanged a warm greeting with an older, handsome and fit-looking man who stepped into their path.

"That was a nasty piece of business out there on the street," the man said.

Cilla remembered that he'd been one of the customers outside earlier. He was about Jonah's height, dark-haired with gray at his temples. He reminded Cilla of a well-aging James Bond. She saw both concern and worry in the steel-colored eyes when they met hers. "Nice work." Then he turned back to Jonah. "What can I do to help?"

"Got it covered," Jonah assured him. "Cilla Michaels, I'd like you to meet Carl Rockwell. Not only is he a regular here at Pleasures, but he was one of my original backers when I opened the club. He believed in me when I was an unknown quantity."

"And I still do," Carl said.

Jonah smiled at him. "He's invested in all my clubs, and now he's a partner in a new place we're opening in San Diego."

Cilla held out a hand and found it firmly grasped.

"Cilla heads up G.W. Securities here in the city," Jonah continued, "and I seem to be her newest client."

"Good." Carl stared directly into Cilla's eyes. "Don't let anyone hurt him, and let me know if you can use some backup."

"He's not kidding," Jonah said. "Before he retired, Carl worked in the security business."

"Virgil can let me know if you need me," Carl said, nodding at the two of them before he returned to the bar.

Jonah led her to an empty booth at the far end of the room. Virgil managed to reach it just as they did.

He beamed a smile at them, then spoke in a low

voice. "Does that little sideshow the two of you put on in the street have anything to do with the green box that was delivered here yesterday?"

"Jury's out on that," Jonah murmured. "I received another box in Denver this morning."

"Shit," Virgil breathed. "What can I do?"

"Exactly what you're doing. Run Pleasures."

Cilla studied the two men as Jonah laid a hand on Virgil's arm and reassured him with the same information he'd given to Carl Rockwell. But he didn't tell either man that he was definitely her client. "I seem to be" just didn't make the cut.

She guessed that Virgil had about a decade on Jonah, and from the easy way they talked, she figured their relationship was personal as well as professional. Plus, Virgil was sharp. He'd already tried to connect the dots between the little Christmas gift Jonah had received and the attack.

Virgil turned to her. "If you work for Gabe Wilder, I have to assume you're the best. What you did out on the street was impressive. But keep it up. Don't let anything happen to Jonah." Then he turned and moved back to the bar.

"Well, I've been well and duly threatened," Cilla said as she slid into the back of the booth. "You have some very concerned friends. Does anyone else here know about the green boxes?"

Jonah shook his head. "Just Virgil. I asked him to keep an eye out in case another was delivered here."

From her position at the back of the booth, Cilla had a view of the entire room. The crowd had thinned a bit so it was the first time that she was able to get a good look at the decor. And since a table now separated her from Jonah, she could give her surroundings more attention than she had on her tour.

The rich combination of dark mahogany and gleaming brass on the bar itself was repeated in the furniture and in the wood panels and sconces that lined the walls. The booths were red leather and the candle flickered in an old-fashioned hurricane lamp.

"What do you think?" Jonah asked.

"Sumptuous. It reminds me of another era where life moved more slowly, before airplanes, when people had the time to travel on a luxury liner to Europe. I got the same impression earlier when I looked up at the second-story windows. It makes me think of the times F. Scott Fitzgerald or Henry James captured in their novels."

He nodded. "That's exactly what we're going for here. Although we don't expect every one of our customers to name the era or to have read those particular authors."

"You have, I bet," Cilla guessed. "What was your major in college?"

"Marketing and Finance, but I minored in English Lit. How about you?"

"Psychology, but I like to read. And I minored in Criminal Justice to pave my way into the police academy."

"You were a cop?" he asked. Then he said, "Here in San Francisco. That's how you know Detective Finelli."

"Right."

"Why'd you leave?"

"Greener pastures. Plus I had a five-year plan. Get some experience in providing personal security and then open up my own office."

Jonah's eyes narrowed. "And running Gabe's satellite office in San Francisco is part of your five-year plan?"

"It is now."

Cilla was prevented from giving him more details when Virgil once more appeared at the side of the table. "What can I get for you?"

Jonah met her eyes. "You mentioned champagne earlier. Does that still sound good?"

"Perfect."

He nodded to Virgil. "We'll have number thirty-five."

For one moment, Cilla let herself wish that the circumstances were different, that she was just sitting at a booth in the bar with an exceptionally handsome man, having a drink. If only there weren't those threatening notes and her decision that Jonah Stone was off-limits, she could have nothing more on her mind than spending another long sexy night with him.

When Virgil moved away, she reluctantly forced her mind back to reality. "I'm not sure what we're celebrating. I need to tell you what Gabe advises."

"I got the gist of it—24/7 protection. But I make my own decisions."

She frowned at him. "He warned me you have an independent streak, but you're not stupid. You have to be willing to hire private security—at least until we figure out what's going on here."

"I'm willing to hire private security."

"But...?" She leaned forward. "I hear a *but* in there. G.W. Securities is the best. And Gabe is your friend. Mark Gibbons and David Santos are the two most experienced agents I have working here in San Francisco. Gabe's even thinking of sending a couple of men in from the Denver office."

"He can stop thinking about that right now."

"I don't..."

Virgil's appearance had her letting the sentence trail off. While he performed all the rituals surrounding the opening of a champagne bottle and filled two flutes, she marshaled her thoughts. Logic would be the path to take.

The instant Jonah signaled his approval of the wine and Virgil walked away, she said, "You need the best. There's more going on here than is immediately apparent."

"What do you mean?"

"The notes you received yesterday and this morning don't jibe with what went down tonight. Whoever sent them is trying for a cat and mouse game. They've set up a ticking-clock scenario—'so many nights and counting...' They want you to worry, anticipate." She waved a hand. "You canceled your plans in Denver and flew back here. What do you want to bet that you'll get another note soon that will have you flying back to Denver?"

His brows quirked upward. "I hadn't thought of that."

She tapped a finger on the table. "That's why you need some pros—to think that way."

Jonah studied her. There was determination in her eyes. Priscilla's eyes, he decided. Logical, focused and a lighter shade of green. Would she taste different if he kissed her now? He was going to find out, he promised himself. But for the moment, he said, "Go on."

"The ticking clock agenda doesn't fit with the guys the police just hauled away. They're grab and go. Instant gratification. They just don't make a match with that note and the Christmasy way it was wrapped up."

"I agree. But it's hard to believe that I have two different people who are out to spoil my holiday."

"True. But we need to consider the possibility. And that's exactly why you have to see the wisdom of hiring G.W. Securities. We have the manpower to check it out."

"I wouldn't hire anyone but G.W. Securities." Then he smiled and lifted his glass. "But if I'm taking on a personal bodyguard, 24/7, you're the one I'm hiring. Not Mark Gibbons or David Santos or anyone Gabe wants to send down from Denver. I want the best of the best."

He tapped his glass to hers. "And didn't you already assure me that's you?"

6

WHILE HER MIND RACED, Cilla took a sip of her champagne. Then for a moment, she allowed herself to be totally distracted by the taste. "This is really good."

"It's the best."

Looking down, she inspected the tiny bubbles. "Don't tell me number thirty-five is that really, really expensive stuff that retails for a few hundred bucks a bottle."

Jonah winced. "The winemakers who bottle Cristal would shudder to hear it described that way."

"Well, I don't think I've ever tasted anything better."

"That's their goal, and they charge a lot when they achieve it."

Looking up, Cilla couldn't prevent the smile and felt a little flutter right below her belly when he returned it. "You didn't have to order something like this. I don't have what they refer to as an educated palate."

"I disagree. You knew right away that it was special. And you did say you've been thinking for some time of dressing up and coming into Pleasures for a drink. Just think of the Cristal as part of your side trip into a different world."

Cinderella-land, she reminded herself. With a very dangerous gatekeeper. Who was now a client. Her current job was to convince Jonah Stone that she could do a better job for him if she kept her distance.

But the more time she spent with him, the more she thought of what she could have—what they both could have—if she closed that distance. And looking into his eyes didn't help one bit because he was thinking the same thing. For an instant, everything around her faded, the noise, the decor, and there was only Jonah.

He was the only one.

No. A sliver of fear shot up her spine. He couldn't be. She wouldn't let him. Her mother had believed that each and every time she'd walked down the aisle. Ruthlessly, Cilla tore her gaze from his and took one more sip out of the glass. It truly was better than any champagne she'd ever tasted. And something she would never be able to afford again. That little reality check gave her back her focus.

Then she met Jonah's eyes. "If you want me to work on this case personally, you have to let me do it my way. The best way that I can protect you is to keep my distance."

"Explain."

This was always the tough part in handling a client—knowing which buttons to push. "You're a businessman. What does your schedule look like tomorrow?"

Jonah pulled out his phone, tapped it a few times and said, "What's your cell phone number?"

When she gave it to him, he said, "I'm sending it to you right now."

"Give me the highlights."

"Since I was still supposed to be in Denver, my

morning is free. But now that I'm back in town, I'll drop by Interludes, my sports club, around lunchtime. They're hosting a Christmas party for the boys and girls clubs here in the city. Later, I have a meeting here at the St. Francis Hotel with Carl Rockwell and Stanley Rubin. Stanley is my other partner in the San Diego club we're opening. He's in town to visit family, and there's a problem he wants to discuss. I'll end my day here at Pleasures. We're busy with parties this time of year."

"How about the rest of the week?"

"There's a charity event at Pleasures the night after tomorrow. I'll be attending."

She frowned. "That isn't a good idea."

"Not negotiable. I'm hosting the event. Bring in some of the cavalry, if you want."

"I *will* want. And something like that is all the more reason for me to assign someone else to you."

When he opened his mouth, she held up a hand. "Let me finish. As a businessman, you know the importance of looking at the whole picture. That's what I'll be doing, and in that position, I'll be free to run down any leads that might turn up, knowing that you're fully protected."

"I don't see why you can't manage that while you're with me. That way you can keep me constantly updated on the big picture. I'm going to insist on that."

She tilted her head to one side and studied him. The glint of humor in his eyes told her that he was being difficult on purpose. And he was enjoying it. Truth told, so was she. She liked matching wits with him. But with Jonah, she had to do more than match. She had to win. So she folded her hands in front of her and met his gaze head-on. "You need someone at your side who can be objective and won't be distracted. Because of our history and the fact that I'm seriously attracted to you, I'm not the best person for that job."

He took a sip of champagne and set the glass down. "How seriously?"

She tapped a finger on the table. "See? That's not the question you should be asking."

"I'll ask another one as soon as you answer—how *seriously* are you attracted to me?"

"Seriously enough that for a moment when you were holding me in your arms out on the street, my mind went blank. There were two guys approaching, one of them was armed, and all I could think of was that I wanted you to kiss me and that I wanted to kiss you right back. That's a serious problem."

"A mutual one. Maybe we should just get it out of our systems."

The humorous glint in his eyes turned reckless and dark. The color made her think of the black smoke that explodes with a spray of sparks from the flames of a bonfire. Hot and dangerous. For the first time in her life, she thought she knew why a moth might be stupid enough to fly into a flame.

She had to fight past the dryness in her throat. "Kissing you again is not going to solve anything."

He moved quickly then, sliding out of his side of the booth and into hers. Without touching her, he studied her for a moment. "You're not afraid."

"No." That was a lie. She was, just a little. Annoyance added to the mix of everything else she was feeling. He was so close now that she could smell him above the scents in the restaurant. Soap and water and something that was very male. Everything inside her began to melt.

He took a strand of her hair and twisted it around his finger. "You're not my type."

She frowned. "Ditto. You're at the top of my Forbidden Fruit list."

"Isn't forbidden fruit even better the second time around? Maybe that's why I've been wanting to taste you again ever since I saw you leaning against my car at the airport."

When his gaze dropped to her mouth, Cilla could feel her lips actually burn. Good glory, she could only pray they still worked. "Look," she managed. "Let me work this case the way I want to and we won't have this problem. You won't have to worry about wanting to kiss Mark or David. I guarantee it."

He laughed, a rich, deep sound that helped her to ease back just a little.

"You're probably right about that." He fastened those razor-sharp eyes on hers. "You strike me as a practical, focused woman. What we shared in that hotel room might have been a fluke."

Her brows shot up. "A fluke with a hell of a lot of chemistry that made us both do things…"

"Delightful things."

"Things that were unwise."

"If I had a dollar for every unwise thing I've ever done…" His lips curved.

And she shouldn't be watching those lips. She took a deep breath and tried to focus. "The chemistry between us hasn't died down, and you're insisting we work together 24/7?"

"Exactly." He lowered his head just a little. "And I think we ought to find out exactly what we're up against so we can handle it."

She wanted to handle it all right. She wanted to

handle *him*. Naked. And dammit, he'd boxed her in. She could smell him, nearly taste him, and she couldn't shove past him without touching him.

And if she touched him? Oh, hell…

"Handle this," she said as she clasped the sides of his head and drew his mouth to hers.

At last. At last. At last.

Those were the words that steamed through Jonah's mind and thrummed in his veins. The memories that had haunted his dreams for the past weeks vanished in the reality of the moment. How could he have forgotten how soft her lips were? Her flavor was even more exciting than he'd recalled. And the sweetness—surely that was new. It reminded him of ice cream that ran down a cone in the summer heat so that you couldn't lick it fast enough.

When she opened for him, he used tongue and teeth to take them both deeper. He couldn't have said who moved first. All he knew was that her strong, slender body was molded to his in a perfect fit. He couldn't seem to get enough of it as he ran his hands down her sides, then up again to cup her breasts.

The low sound of desperation she made in her throat had his blood racing like a river just before it tumbled over the falls. He knew what it was like to throw caution to the winds, but he'd never wanted so badly to do just that.

He wanted to touch her. No, he needed to touch her, to strip her out of that dress and explore the skin beneath, inch by inch by inch. More than that, he wanted to have her now, right here.

Not possible, he warned himself. He wasn't so far gone that he'd lost track of his surroundings. Not yet.

But he couldn't seem to control his hands, couldn't seem to give up her taste.

Even when glass shattered nearby, he had to exert some effort to pull away. And it took even more discipline to drop his hands and ease back from her.

Her eyes were still clouded. And her mouth…

He only had to look at it for the intensity of his desire to spike again. No other woman had ever taken him as far as she had. And he wanted to experience—no, he needed to experience—just how much further they could take each other. He met her eyes. "Come with me now."

"No." But she didn't retreat from him. "I didn't kiss you and you didn't kiss me as a prelude to seduction. We did it to clarify the problem. And I'd say mission accomplished. Now you have to agree that I should work this case from a distance. That way we can both think."

"Distance won't solve the problem of what we're thinking about. And thinking about making love again while we're apart might prove even more of a distraction."

Cilla waited three beats, then sighed. "Compromise time."

He smiled at her. "I'm ready to negotiate, as long as you're my personal bodyguard until we figure out what's going on."

"And stop it."

His expression sobered. "Yes."

"We need some ground rules. I don't sleep with clients—as much as I might want to. Or as much as the client might want me to. During the last job I worked in L.A., the client believed our security service should provide some side benefits."

He caught her hand. "I'm sorry."

"I don't want you to be sorry. I want you to understand. Whatever it is we've got going between us has to take a backseat until we figure out who's sending those notes."

"We can put what we're feeling in the backseat. That doesn't mean it will stay there."

She saw the humor in his eyes again, and it didn't help that she had quite a vivid image of the two of them in the backseat of a car, their limbs tangled. It helped even less that she knew he was thinking the same thing, and she had no one to blame but herself for the expression.

"Look. We're both adults. We stayed away from each other for nearly a month. From now until we get your note sender, our relationship has to be strictly professional—security agent and client."

"It's a reasonable ground rule. I'll agree with one modification. I won't be sidelined. I want to be kept informed of everything you know, and I want to be part of running down leads. I don't like threats, and if I'm not working with you, I'll be working on my own. Until this is over, we're partners."

"Gabe won't like it."

"Gabe will have to live with it. Will you?"

"As long as we agree that when it comes to any kind of imminent threat, I take the lead."

"Unless I have a better idea."

"We won't always have time for negotiations," she warned.

"True. But I followed your lead earlier this evening. And there is a chance that I might on occasion have a better idea."

Since it was the best deal she was going to get, she nodded. "Okay. But I'm going to take the lead on this one. I'm going to have someone from G.W. Securities outside watching when I leave tonight."

"Agreed."

She took out her cell and checked the schedule he'd sent her. "And if we're going to be working on this together, I get to go where you go—everywhere you go, including business meetings."

He grinned at her. "You're going to cause quite a stir in the men's room."

"Not funny. You need to decide how you're going to explain me to your partners, Stanley Rubin and Carl Rockwell, when I show up with you at the St. Francis Hotel tomorrow. Unless you want them to know about your problem."

The reminder didn't wipe the grin from his face, but it did make his eyes darken. And it only took him a few beats to come up with a solution.

"Carl Rockwell already knows you're from G.W. Securities, and I'll tell Stanley I'm taking precautions because of the attempted mugging." He refilled their glasses, then handed her one before he raised his in a toast. "Now let's drink to *our* partnership."

LESS THAN EIGHT HOURS later, Cilla stood with Jonah looking through a two-way glass as Detective Joe Finelli questioned the man she'd kicked with her red shoe. They'd already watched his interview with the skinny guy, Lorenzo Rossi. Chubby's name was Mickey Pastori, known to his friends as Mickey P., and the shiner he was sporting paid tribute to the punch she'd given him. The public defender assigned to his case looked tired—as if she'd been rousted out of bed at a very early hour.

Cilla could sympathize with that since she'd gotten

the call from Detective Finelli at 7:00 a.m. Both Rossi and Pastori had consulted with their Public Defenders and claimed they wanted to cooperate. She'd debated notifying Jonah, but a deal was a deal. He'd been very explicit about wanting to be in on everything.

So he was here right now in an observation room listening to Joe Finelli tell Mickey P. to take it from the top one more time.

She flicked a glance at Jonah's reflection in the glass that looked into the interrogation room. His attention seemed totally focused on Mickey P. She wished it were that easy for her to concentrate on the interrogation. But she was so aware of him standing only inches away from her. Each time she took a breath, she inhaled his scent. And if he made a move to touch her…

No. The problem was that after a night on her couch—a night in which Jonah Stone had invaded her dreams every time she'd managed to slip into sleep— she was the one who wanted to touch him.

"I don't know nuthin'," Mickey P. whined.

"I still need to hear it from the top again," Finelli said.

Cilla shifted her gaze back to the interrogation room. She'd worked with partners before, and she'd find a way to work with Jonah Stone. Or around him. And she wasn't going to let her thoughts stray to being wrapped around him, or underneath him.

Stop it. Ruthlessly, she shoved the images out of her mind. He was following her ground rules. So far, he'd even let her take the lead. Last night, he'd allowed her to check out his apartment, including the security, and this morning he'd waited for her knock on his door before he'd opened it and stepped out. He'd offered no objection when she'd insisted that they use her car to get to the police station. In short, he was being Mr. Perfect Client.

She looked over at his reflection again. This time he met her eyes in the glass. And any idea of Jonah as a client, perfect or not, vanished. There was such heat in his gaze that she was amazed it didn't burn a hole right through the glass. And everything else suddenly faded just as it had the first time he'd looked at her.

"This is not working." He took her arm and turned her before she could think. Before she could breathe.

"I need a kiss," he said as he framed her face with his hands. "Give me one."

Heat flooded her system and her mind began to empty. The man had fast moves. She should have remembered that. "But…ground rules."

"You'll have to agree, I've followed them so far."

"Yes." She had to move. But the brain cells that controlled motion had evidently been the first ones to shut off. His were still working. He'd gripped her shoulders and somehow moved her against the wall.

"I should get points for being good so far. And if I'm going to listen to one more word of Mickey P.'s whining excuses, I need a reward."

Then his mouth was on hers. The kiss was hard, demanding, everything she'd been imagining since the last time. She couldn't think, no longer remembered that she should. Suddenly, she could move again. Her arms wrapped around him and she pressed closer. She had to get closer.

Yes, Jonah thought as he molded her against the wall. The desire to kiss her had been building since she'd picked him up at his apartment. No—since she'd left the night before. And as they'd stood in the tiny observation room watching Joe Finelli question the two thugs, desire had intensified until he needed the kiss the way a starving man needed food, or a man dying of thirst needed water. He didn't understand it. He wasn't sure he wanted to.

What he wanted was Cilla. Only Cilla. He ran his hands down her quickly, wishing he had more time, taking what he could get. But when he heard Finelli's voice again from the interrogation room, he pulled back. If he didn't, he was afraid he wouldn't be able to.

Still, he couldn't completely let her go. For one more moment, he held her close and rested his forehead against hers. "Thanks," he managed. "Now I'll go back to being good again."

For how long? If she'd been sure her voice was working, Cilla would have asked the question out loud. But there was a part of her that didn't want him to be good. As Jonah moved away, she concentrated on making sure her legs carried her back to the glass window.

Inside the room, Mickey P. said, "Lorenzo is the one you should be talking to. I just agreed to go along because of the money. Easy-peasy. That's the way Lorenzo described the job. Five hundred in advance and another five when the job was done."

As he whined on, his story didn't change. The driver of the van had hired them. Mickey P. didn't even know who the guy was except that he called himself Tank. They were to wait for Jonah Stone to arrive at his club and rough him up a bit.

"No one was supposed to be with him," Mickey P. complained to Finelli.

"Several witnesses saw your pal, the driver, take a shot at Mr. Stone," Finelli said.

"I don't know nuthin' 'bout that," Mickey P. insisted. "Shooting Stone was not part of the deal."

"Then why did you bring a gun and threaten Mr. Stone with it?"

"If he'd been alone, I wouldn't have had to use the gun. We were just going to scare him, take him into the alley and punch him a few times. But we had to get the woman out of the way. Then she kicked me."

"Spoilsport," Jonah murmured beside her.

"All part of the service." She didn't look at him. She didn't dare. And she wasn't going to look at his reflection, either.

"Think Mickey P.'s telling the truth?"

Cilla considered that. Lorenzo Rossi had claimed just as much ignorance as Mickey P. He only knew the driver of the van as Tank. A tall, broad-shouldered guy with a gray buzz cut had walked into a bar where he and Mickey usually hung out and hired them for a dream job. All they had to do was rough up Jonah and the payoff was one grand. Both Mickey P. and Lorenzo had rap sheets, but they were small-time.

"What's your gut instinct?" Jonah prompted.

In the room in front of her, Mickey P. groaned about a headache.

"I think they're both essentially telling the truth. Joe will keep after them for a while, and Lorenzo may eventually remember more about this Tank person. But something about their story rings true."

She looked at him then. "What does your gut tell you?"

"Same thing," he said without hesitation. "Neither one of them are Einsteins. They went for the easy money. Neither of them counted on you, and neither has the ability to think on their feet."

"That would jibe with my take on it," Detective Finelli said.

They both turned to him as he entered the room. "Except I wouldn't mention either of them in the same sentence with Einstein. I've got a couple of men calling other precincts to see if anyone's heard of this Tank. I'm thinking he's pretty small-time, too. And the license plates on the van are a dead end. They were reported stolen yesterday afternoon."

"So the large man with the short gray hair who goes by 'Tank' could be behind the notes or he could be working for someone else," Cilla said. "And since Skinny and Fatso are a few bologna sandwiches short of a picnic, we're probably not any closer to finding out who that person is, or if Tank's behind everything."

Finelli shot a grin at Jonah. "She's real good at summarizing the bad news. How about you? You've had all night to think about it. You got any thoughts about who sent the notes?"

Jonah had given it some thought. He'd had no choice since Cilla had assigned him to make a list of anyone he might remember who could have a grudge against him going back to the days when he'd been in foster care. But his mind had frequently slipped back to Cilla. In fact he wasn't sure whether it was the note or the woman standing beside him that had stolen more of his sleep. He felt a little better now that he'd kissed her, but he wasn't at all sure how long he could wait to do it again.

"I've made a list for Cilla of people who might have it in for me, but I don't think the note sender is on it. None of them feel right. We'll just have to keep working on it. What's next?"

Finelli inclined his head toward the glass. "I'll keep

working on them. And we'll keep looking for the van. If you want to hang around, I can offer you both some very bad coffee." He grinned at Cilla. "But if I remember correctly, that's one of the reasons you quit being a cop and went private."

"One of many," Cilla said. "I'm going to take Jonah to G.W. Securities so we can discuss what we know and strategize. The coffee's excellent there." Then she gave Finelli a hug. "Thanks for letting us watch. I'd appreciate it if you'd keep me posted."

"Ditto," Finelli said. Then he nodded at Jonah. "You're working with the best."

Jonah didn't need convincing. As they threaded their way through the desks in the bull pen, he noted that a couple of the uniforms waved at her. That didn't surprise him. As soon as she'd left his apartment the night before, he'd given in to the temptation to check into her background—something he'd avoided doing for nearly a month. She'd put in three years on the SFPD and she seemed to be well liked here.

He'd also checked into the agency she'd worked for in L.A. It was small and specialized in providing discreet personal security for celebrity clients. He'd also located the story Gabe had told him about the client whose life she'd saved. But there'd been nothing about the one who'd expected side benefits.

"So, besides the lure of greener pastures, better coffee and your five-year plan, why did you go the Charlie's Angels' route and move to L.A.?"

She laughed then. "Don't I wish I'd become one of Charlie's Angels. They always looked like they were having such fun. They got interesting cases, they got to go undercover and they always had Charlie and Bosley watching their backs. Maybe I had that in mind, but the real world is very different. Mostly I got to babysit the spoiled teen idol crowd."

He took her arm and waited until she met his eyes. "Was it one of the teens who wanted side benefits?"

"Yeah. But he didn't get them, and that case is history. Plus, I got a better offer from Gabe."

Her tone was offhand, but the increased tension in her body told him that was just the surface story. He was willing to bet there was a deeper one. He'd have it when the time was right.

The desk sergeant hailed them as they passed her desk. "Ms. Michaels. A delivery service just left this for Mr. Stone. I saw his name next to yours on the sign-in sheet."

There was a coldness in Jonah's gut as he looked at the small green box tied with a red bow.

"What delivery service?" Cilla asked.

"Some private one," the sergeant said. "He asked me to sign a clipboard."

"What did he look like?" Cilla pressed.

"Tall, broad-shouldered, short gray hair. I'd say he was in his late fifties."

"Thanks, Sergeant."

"Sounds like our man Tank." Cilla hurried Jonah quickly into the street and scanned it. Because of the early hour, the pedestrian traffic was thin. "Dammit. There's no sign of him. No sign of that van."

Jonah waited until they were near Cilla's car before he opened the box. Then he lifted out the note and held it so they could read it together.

Four nights and counting... Have you remembered yet why you're going to have to pay? You have some time left. But even in this most joyous of seasons, peaceful interludes are short.

Cilla took out her cell. "I'll let Joe know."

7

SHE WAS RIGHT ABOUT THE coffee, Jonah had to admit. It was very good. She'd poured a generous mug for each of them before she'd excused herself and left him standing in front of her desk.

G.W. Securities occupied the top floor of a modern-looking building. Cilla's corner office offered a spectacular view of the Golden Gate Bridge and was spacious enough to hold a gleaming conference table as well as a cozy sitting area with a leather sofa and two chairs.

Her desk was meticulously clean and bare of any photos or mementos. The office clearly belonged to Priscilla. But on the only solid wall hung a painting where red, yellow and purple pansies exploded in bursts of color. That was Cilla. In the bright colors, he saw a visual representation of the energy that always simmered inside of her.

Initially, it had surprised him that she was an ex-cop. But the part of her that he was coming to think of as Priscilla would have made an excellent cop with her focus and her attention to detail. Before they'd left the police station, she'd checked her car for a bomb. And she'd kept her eye out to see if anyone followed them the short distance to her office. So had he, and he hadn't spotted anyone.

But he also hadn't spotted a tail on the way to the police station. And the Tank person must have followed them. Otherwise, how would he have known to deliver the note there? He didn't like the idea of that, and he had a pretty good idea that she didn't, either.

Through the other three glass walls, he noted some of the staff and agents settling in at their desks. He sipped coffee as he watched her turn the green box with the red ribbon over to Mark Gibbons. She'd introduced him when they'd arrived. Jonah recalled that he was one of the two men she'd wanted to assign to him, but it was only when he'd seen Mark that he'd recognized him as an agent who'd worked for Gabe in the Denver office. Gabe had hired him about six years ago when Jonah had left G.W. Securities to open Pleasures.

Tall with a swimmer's build, Gibbons had thinning hair and a neat goatee that was just beginning to show signs of gray. Cilla was assigning him the task of hand delivering the box and note to a lab G.W. Securities used here in San Francisco.

On the short drive over from the police station, she'd filled Jonah in on her plans to do that much. She'd also put in a call to David Santos, the other agent she'd mentioned. She was going to put him in charge of tracking down the people Jonah had written on his possible enemies list. Locating them would be the first step. If they were alive and well and otherwise occupied, they could be crossed off.

All of which would take time, probably more than his ticking four-night clock would allow them. They hadn't talked about the latest note. Not yet. He was fine with that. Her silence during the drive had given him time to think.

In his mind, he pictured each of the notes. There was something in the messages that he was still missing. Six nights, then five and now four. It was December 21 and kids everywhere had started their countdown to Christmas a long time ago. Why had the writer of the notes waited to begin with day six?

He pushed down hard on both frustration and temper. That was something he'd started training himself to do ever since he'd first met Father Mike and begun what had become a new life. His first day at the center had been early December—sixteen years ago. White lights had twinkled on the trees in the prayer garden that bordered the basketball court. In the center of the tiny garden was a statue that he'd later learned was St. Francis. And it was where the social worker had taken him to meet Father Mike on that first day.

He'd never met a priest before. What he'd expected was someone wearing black who'd lecture him and give him the worn-out lie that good deeds would be rewarded and evil ones punished. In the four years he'd spent in foster care he'd heard that one often enough. Father Mike had been wearing a T-shirt, shorts and sneakers, and instead of a lecture, he'd offered Jonah a game of one-on-one on the basketball court. Within the next fifteen minutes, they'd been joined and then challenged by two other kids—Gabe Wilder and Nash Fortune. The other guys had been good, but he and Father Mike had won.

A smile tugged at the corner of his mouth as he recalled the competition as well as the brownies and milk that had followed. There'd been no lecture, not that day or any other day. The St. Francis Center for Boys had never been about lectures. Now he understood that it had been about giving young boys a place to channel their fear and anger and frustration and, most of all, to have fun and formulate dreams.

His gaze sharpened and his mind returned to Cilla as she began to move back toward her office. Even through the glass wall and the distance that separated them, his senses were attuned to her. He watched her take a circuitous route, pausing on the way twice to speak to people. In addition to protecting him, she still had an office to run, and she looked very much at home checking with her colleagues.

He continued to study her as she took a call on her cell. She wore her hair in a neat braid, but the bright blue blazer spoke of the passion he knew lay beneath the surface. A passion that had drawn him from the first.

He'd had time to think about it during the night, to try to analyze what she was doing to him. It wasn't just desire that she was able to trigger in him. The feeling he got when he looked at her was more complicated, similar to that flash of intuition he experienced when he was drawn to a new business venture. A feeling of rightness.

That was what he'd felt when he'd first seen her, and again during the long night they'd spent together in Denver. He'd never gotten that feeling about a woman before. He'd never wanted to. It was too close to the way his mother had described her first meeting with his father.

As a child, he'd loved to hear the story, especially during his dad's long absences when he'd been away working on secret missions for the government. As his mother told it, they'd met at a fancy party. She'd been a waitress working for the caterers and he'd been a guest. They'd seen each other across a crowded room, and that had been it. Within days, they'd run away to be married. A real Cinderella story—except there hadn't been a happy ever after. Thanks to his father.

He wasn't at all comfortable with the idea that he might have experienced the same feeling his mother had described the night he'd first seen Cilla.

So the smartest thing to do would be to play by her rules and keep their relationship strictly professional.

Then he saw a tall, lanky man stride past the reception area and make a beeline toward Cilla. His long dark hair curled over his ears and reached the collar of his shirt. In the faded jeans and worn leather jacket, he looked as if he'd be more at home on a ranch than in the sleek, modern office.

A vague sense of recognition tugged at Jonah. He rarely forgot a face, and he'd seen the man before. Where? The smile that spread over Cilla's face as she spotted him and the easy way the man returned it left a coppery taste in Jonah's mouth and something twisted in his stomach. He'd taken a step toward the door before he stopped himself.

Jealousy. He'd felt it before, but never about a woman. And no woman had ever triggered this kind of possessiveness before. The kind that made him want to forget all about rules or playing it smart.

She entered the room with the cowboy only a step behind her. "David Santos, this is Jonah Stone."

The other man she'd been going to assign to him, Jonah recalled. Stepping forward, he gripped Santos's outstretched hand. "I've seen you before. Where?"

Santos smiled. "You may have caught a glimpse of

me at one of your clubs, Interludes. Been there a couple of times, and I'll be back. Great place."

"Come anytime." Jonah found himself returning the smile. "Cilla tells me you have the unenviable job of tracking down all my possible enemies. Good luck with that."

"Slight change of plans," Cilla said. "David's going to distribute that task to our staff and from now on he'll follow us around from a distance and provide backup as needed. Gabe thinks it's a good idea."

"I agree." As Jonah looked from Santos to Cilla, he didn't miss the slight easing of tension in her shoulders.

Santos nodded at him. "I'll get started on the traces."

The moment he left the office, Jonah said, "You're reassigning Santos to give us backup because you think someone followed us to the police station."

"How else would they know to deliver the green box there?" A trace of a frown appeared on her forehead. "But I didn't see or sense the tail."

"Neither did I, and I watched." It was his turn to frown. "You're thinking that you didn't sense the tail because I was distracting you."

"That crossed my mind. You made me forget where I was in the police station."

He smiled at her. "I've been good since then. And I haven't seen any indication that you're distracted enough to keep you from doing the job."

"The thing is—I didn't *feel* like we were being followed." She raised a hand to rub the back of her neck. "Usually, I get an itchy feeling. If you're interfering with my instincts, you'd be better—"

He stepped forward as he cut her off. "I was watching, too. What if neither of us sensed or spotted the tail because there wasn't one?"

She frowned. "Then how did your gift giver know to deliver the package to the police precinct?"

"How else would *you* trace the movements of a car?"

"Shit." She fisted her hands on her hips and paced to one of the glass walls and back again. "Some kind of tracking device. And it wouldn't have to be in the places where I checked for a bomb." Whirling, she moved quickly to the door. "Come with me."

She stopped to let Santos know they'd be right back. Then Jonah had to lengthen his stride to keep up with her as she led the way out of the office to the elevator. In two minutes flat, they were at the level where she'd parked. Thirty seconds after that, they stood at the rear of her red sports car. It was now boxed in snugly by two large sedans that had managed to take more than their allotted space between the yellow lines.

"I'll take the driver's side," he said.

She didn't argue. Instead, she squatted down and ran her hand underneath the rear bumper. Nothing. Inching her way forward, she examined the right rear fender. Nothing again. It was the right front fender where her fingers struck pay dirt. "Got it."

She ran her fingers over the object. "It's tiny, maybe three inches long, maybe two wide."

Circling around the back of the car, Jonah joined her and reached under the fender to check it out. "You want me to remove it?"

"No way." She gripped his wrist with her fingers and withdrew his hand with her own. "If we leave it, we may be able to find a use for it."

"Like leading him on a wild-goose chase. I like it."

Turning her head, she smiled at him and found that he was much closer than she'd thought. Their knees were brushing, and his mouth was only a few inches from hers. Awareness shimmered through her.

The quick curve of that mouth and the amusement in his eyes triggered something inside her. Not the heat that she'd felt before, but something warmer and sweeter that spread like a slow-moving river. Fascinated, she wondered how a simple shared smile could be more intimate than the kisses they'd shared. Or the long night they'd spent together in Denver.

She could move back. Oh, she should move back. Because if she wasn't mistaken his mouth had edged just a little bit closer. Her fingers still gripped his wrist, and she felt his pulse jump just as hers was doing.

"I like the way your mind works, Cilla."

"Same goes."

Her pulse jumped again when he freed his wrist and took her hand, linked his fingers with hers. "I want to kiss you again."

"Same goes there, too. But we can't." Still, she didn't move. She was no longer sure she could. She was experiencing that same disconnect between brain and body that she'd felt in the police station. His mouth was closer now, only a breath away. "Rules."

His lips brushed hers. "I've always thought they were meant for bending."

His mouth was on hers. Not hard and demanding as she'd expected, but soft, testing, tasting. There was no pressure, only invitation, and every cell in her body urged her to accept. When he changed the angle, and gently nipped at her bottom lip, she trembled.

He'd never tempted her this way before. No one had. All the lectures she'd given herself during the night and the ride over from the police station were wiped away as her senses sharpened one by one.

There was so much to feel. A chill in the air that contrasted sharply with the warmth of his skin, the heat of his mouth. She smelled the lingering fumes of exhaust, but also caught his scent, soap and something that was unique to him. She heard the rumble of traffic on the street below, the growl of a car's engine on the level above them. And she could hear her own sigh escape as she moved closer and slipped her tongue between his teeth.

His taste seeped into her then, his flavor just as hot and pungent as she remembered. How had she lived through all those long lonely nights without having it again? She kept her eyes open, though she badly wanted to close them, to yield completely to the moment and to him. But she had to see who he was, to understand what there was about this one man that could make her forget everything but him.

It was so wrong to let him do this to her. So dangerous. But she couldn't gather the will to stop. As he deepened the kiss, slowly, persuasively, everything became involved in that mouth-to-mouth contact. She felt not only her body yield but her mind and her heart, as well. The warmth that had spread through her shifted seamlessly into an ache that started to build and sharpen. She laid her free hand on his cheek and tightened the fingers still gripping his hand.

The sound, explosive as a gunshot, had her pushing him down on the cement floor of the garage, covering as much of his body as she could with her own.

"Stay," she ordered in a whisper when he gripped her shoulders. Even as she dug beneath her jacket for her gun, she felt his moment of hesitation.

"My call," she snapped. "Look under the car to your right. Tell me what you see."

Even as he turned his head, she did the same and scanned the area to his left. There was no one approaching on foot in her limited sight line. But she caught the sound of the engine before Jonah said, "Car turning in from the level above."

There was little space to maneuver between the parked cars so she had to wiggle her way far enough up his body in order to grip the gun with both hands.

The vehicle shot past in a blur. A black van with a big man behind the wheel. She would have moved then, but Jonah's arm clamped hard around her waist. Tires squealed as the van took the turn to the lower level, and another loud crack echoed off the walls of the garage.

"Let me go," Cilla said. "It's Tank and our backfiring van. I'd swear to it."

"You're not going to catch him," Jonah said, his breath tickling her cheek. "And last night he had a gun he wasn't afraid to use."

Tires squealed again, and there was the sound of a muffled crash, then a noisy engine speeding up.

"See?" He released her. "It sounds like he didn't even have time to pay his parking ticket."

"Stay put for a minute." Cilla got to her knees, but she didn't reholster her gun until she'd risen to her feet and scanned the parking area. Nothing moved. The only sound came from traffic on the street below.

She glanced back down at him. He looked very relaxed lying there on the cement floor. And there was a part of her that wanted very badly to join him. Another part of her wanted to imagine in great detail what they might have been doing if the backfiring van hadn't interrupted them.

Firmly, she latched onto the part of her that had a job to do. "This might have been worse." She didn't like to think about that. She hadn't taken into consideration that someone could have been waiting in the garage for them. She certainly hadn't been thinking about work when Jonah had kissed her. "There are very important reasons not to bend the rules. From now on, we're going to follow them."

He grinned up at her. "Don't I even get some points for following orders and letting you take the lead?"

"That's one of the rules."

He held up a hand. "How about helping me up."

She shot him her sweetest smile. "Not when you're still thinking about helping me down."

"Can't blame a guy for trying." Jonah rolled and had one palm pressed to the ground and one knee under him when he suddenly lowered his head and peered more intently beneath her car. "What have we here?"

"What is it?"

When he met her eyes this time, the amusement had faded from his. "I'm no expert, but my guess is that there's a bomb on your rear axle."

8

HALF AN HOUR LATER, JONAH followed Cilla into a coffee shop two blocks down from her office building. Janine's. Cilla had suggested the place to him when the officer heading up the bomb squad informed her it would be another half hour or so before he could clear the garage and her office building for reentry.

Janine's was small, not part of a chain, with red-checkered tablecloths and miniature poinsettia plants on each table. The music was instrumental and muted, featuring a saxophone crooning "Silent Night." The air was rich with the scents of bacon, coffee and cinnamon.

A pretty waitress in her late-twenties approached them. "Your usual table, Ms. Michaels?"

"That would be great, Janine."

Not merely a waitress, Jonah mused, but young to be the owner.

"There's a lot of excitement down the block," Janine said. "Fire engines, police cars."

"Bomb scare in the garage of my building," Cilla told her. "Someone phoned it in. It's all being taken care of, but they had to evacuate everyone temporarily. It's just a precaution."

"Well, jeez," Janine said, then added, "My grandmother says Christmas always brings out the crazies."

"How is your grandmother?" Cilla asked.

"Great. She's totally annoyed that she can't come in here seven days a week. But she manages two or three. She doesn't trust my mom and me to make the cinnamon buns right."

They followed her to a table at the back where they could both sit with a view of the door and the street.

At Cilla's instructions, David Santos had followed them and chosen a table closer to the door. Gibbons, who'd returned to the building just as the first police cruisers had arrived, was going to check the security discs just as soon as the building was cleared.

Cilla had a point about sticking to the ground rules. Jonah was more than willing to concede that as he ordered coffee from Janine. It was the main reason he'd let her slip totally into the role of security agent since he'd spotted that bomb.

If that car hadn't backfired and jerked him back into reality, he'd have done more than bend the rules in the parking garage. They'd have made love right there only a few inches away from the bomb. While she'd been placing phone calls to her office and the police, he'd used the time to leash in the fury and the fear that had gripped him tight in the belly when he'd seen the wires hanging from the underside of her car.

She'd been a cop, he'd reminded himself. And the Priscilla part of her believed in following procedures. So she'd have checked the car before she'd driven anywhere in it. She'd have found the bomb. That conviction was strengthened by the methodical way she'd contacted Finelli and Gabe before they'd even left the garage.

"You're angry," she said.

"Damn straight. That bastard planted a bomb under your car. But I know temper is never the answer."

She met his eyes. "I agree. What we need to do is focus all of our attention on discovering who is behind the notes."

The chilly, almost lecturing tone of her voice had him wanting to smile. "In other words, I'm the client and you're the pro."

"Yes."

Tilting his head, he studied her. She'd been pulling back from him ever since he'd spotted the bomb. He was beginning to suspect there wasn't going to be any backing away for either of them. But he could be patient when he wanted to be.

"Fine. We still can't be sure if this Tank person is working alone or if he's been hired by someone else. Sometimes the best way to figure out the who is to discover the why."

She pulled a legal pad and a pencil out of the bag Santos had brought her when he'd joined them in the garage. "I think better when I'm writing—or at least scribbling."

"You mind sharing? I'm a bit of a doodler myself."

She ripped off some sheets and fished out another pencil. Then she grabbed her cell, flicked the screen a few times with her finger. "According to the text you sent me with your schedule, we're not due at Interludes for another hour. And you have a meeting with your partners, Carl Rockwell and Stanley Rubin, at the St. Francis Hotel at four-thirty."

"That's correct."

"From now on we'll use taxis," she said. "While we have some time, I'd like to ask you some questions that

I was going to ask in the office earlier. They're the same ones I'd ask any client that came to me with a problem like yours."

Jonah decided he'd been playing the role of "good client" too long. "I'd like to start by discussing this." On one of the sheets she'd given him, he wrote *td*. Then he held it so she could read the letters.

"'Td'?"

"I'm wondering when that little tracking device was put on your car?"

She pursed her lips and thought for a moment. "My guess is that it was last night when I was with you at Pleasures."

"So our friend Tank must have revisited the scene of the crime after his getaway and planted it then. Gutsy bastard."

"Yes. The van was parked across the street from the parking lot. He would have seen us drive in. He'd know my car."

"He couldn't have been happy with the way you interfered. So he puts a tracking device on your car, and now he probably knows who you are."

"And your point is?"

There was an edge to her tone, and he liked it a lot better than the chilly, lecturing one. "We're not merely security expert and client. We're partners, and you may need someone to watch your back as much as I do."

"David Santos is watching both of our backs." She leaned closer, the edge in her voice sharpening even as she lowered it. "As soon as Mark brings us what he's found on the garage's security discs, he'll join the team. So I think you should remember that you are the client and let me do my job."

Janine appeared with their coffees and a plate of cinnamon buns. "They're on the house." She was shaking her head as she walked off. "Bomb scares four days before Christmas."

As soon as she was out of earshot, Jonah said, "Your eyes get darker when you're angry but not as dark as when I'm kissing—"

"Stop!" She hissed the word as she poked a finger into his shoulder. "Stop that right now or you'll be proving that I was right all along and David and Mark should be sitting here, not me. We should not have been doing…what we were doing in that garage."

"Maybe not." He took a strand of her hair, tested the silkiness between his fingers. "I'm not sure we can prevent…what we were doing…from happening again."

"Backseat rule," she reminded him. "Let me do my job."

"Okay." He leaned away from her. "I'll go back to playing good client for a while on one condition."

She shot up a brow. "What?"

"You're staying at my place tonight."

"Why should I do that?"

"The tracking device and bomb were put on *your* car. This guy has gotten you in his sights. If we stay together, we can make better use of G.W. Securities' resources. Hopefully, we can prevent more people on your staff from becoming targets."

He pulled out his cell phone. "Until this is over, we're together, 24/7. I can make that argument to Gabe right now if you'd like."

Cilla frowned at him while her mind raced for an alternative argument. But dammit, he was right. Gabe would not only agree with him but wonder why she didn't. "I can see why you're good at negotiating deals."

He smiled at her. "I'm good at other things, too." He

gripped her chin in his hand and gave her a brief kiss. At least, he'd intended it to be brief. But that intention flew out the window when her lips softened and opened for him, and her taste lured him into taking more. Each time he kissed her, there seemed to be more flavors to explore—layers of sweetness and spice that changed as the heat grew.

He'd expected her to pull back. But she had yet to do that. And the thought, the challenge of it had him adjusting the slant of the kiss and plunging them both deeper. The flavors changed again. Now what he tasted was a mix of surrender and greed, and he was no longer sure that he had the power to pull back. He sank fast, further and further until something inside of him gave way.

He was vaguely aware of a smattering of applause, a couple of whistles. But that wasn't what gave him the strength to draw away. It was the realization that this woman might be able to take everything from him. Everything.

Jonah leaned back in his chair and reminded himself to breathe. His head was still spinning but he managed to keep his hand steady when he reached for one of the buns.

He took a bite, watching her and waiting for her eyes to clear before he pointed at the plate Janine had brought. "We're going to need another order of these. Suddenly, I'm starved."

Cilla spoke in a very low voice. "You were supposed to play good client."

"I tried."

"Try harder." She lifted her pencil. "This is a question I would ask any client during a first session so don't give me any grief. How exactly would you describe what's happening to you? I want it in your own words."

He sipped his coffee again. She had to have been as affected by that kiss as he was, and he admired the way she could snap right back into Priscilla mode. But it had been Cilla he'd kissed. Cilla who was as vulnerable to him as he was to her.

"I'm not asking for a novel here or a dissertation," she said, "just a short description, twenty-five words or less."

The thread of sarcasm in her tone had him smiling. "Someone has sent me three mildly threatening notes all wrapped up as Christmas presents. And they hired some rather incompetent thugs to mug me."

"Why 'mildly' threatening?"

He paused long enough to bite into another bun, chew and swallow. "Because the notes aren't specific, I suppose. Reminding me that life and fortune are fleeting doesn't amount to a death threat. Life and fortune *are* fleeting. Everything can be lost in a heartbeat."

"But they also want you to pay."

"For what? Even that's vague. Maybe the notes are leading up to some kind of ransom demand."

She tapped her pencil on the pad. "For money?"

"Yes."

"And the attempted mugging, the bomb planted under my car are geared to scare you and motivate you to pay." She considered for a moment. "None of the people on the list you gave me rings a bell yet?"

"Not a one."

Cilla studied him closely. "Any ex-lovers who might hold a grudge?"

He smiled again. And just that sudden curve of his

lips softened her bones. She could no longer feel the pencil she held in her hand.

"No complaints so far," he said.

There wouldn't be. Cilla certainly didn't have any. And she didn't seem to have any resistance to him. Not in the garage earlier and not when he'd kissed her a few minutes ago. It didn't matter where they were when he kissed her, she wanted. Nothing, no one else existed but him. It was that simple. That terrifying.

A man who could kiss the way he did could probably ease his way out of a relationship as easily as he indulged in one. With no hard feelings on anyone's part. Wasn't that exactly the deal he'd offered her in that hotel bar? The thought brought the feeling back to her fingers.

"And the use of words like *pleasures* and *interludes,* names of your clubs—does that seem mildly threatening also?"

He frowned. "Yes. And more specific in a way."

She glanced up and met his eyes again. "Your businesses mean a lot to you."

"Yes."

Although it was the answer she expected to hear, Cilla felt a tightening around her heart. To a man like Jonah Stone, the businesses he'd created would take precedence over everything. That had always been the case with her father.

Then she refocused. "You're more worried about the threat to your clubs than you are about the possible threat to you."

There was a beat before he said, "Yes."

"Who would know that about you?"

He thought for a moment. "My close friends, anyone

who works for me. Perhaps even anyone I've done business with."

"A manager like Virgil would certainly be aware of this. How about the manager of Interludes?"

"Carmen D'Annunzio. Yes, she would. She volunteered at the St. Francis Center my last year there when opening Pleasures was on my mind 24/7. Her two sons were regulars. I thought of her a few years later when I opened Interludes and she agreed to move here to San Francisco."

"I'll want to talk to Virgil and Carmen. They could have valuable insights." After jotting down the names, she glanced at him again. "It would be better if I could speak with them alone."

"We'll be at both places today. I can give you some time with them."

"What about your family?"

"I don't have one."

The sudden coolness in his tone was a perfect match to what she saw in his eyes. He wanted her to back off.

She kept her voice calm, her tone reasonable. "Everyone has a family, even if we'd rather trade them in for different models. Gabe wouldn't have to ask the question because he probably already knows. But I don't, and you insisted that I work the case. What happened to your family?"

He said nothing for a moment. "I'll tell you about my family if you'll tell me about yours."

She bit back a sigh. "I'm not asking you to satisfy idle curiosity. Finding out about your family is part of my job."

He nodded. "A job you're good at, so you must have to negotiate with difficult clients. I don't like to talk about my family. So if I have to dig them up, what can it hurt to humor me a little?"

She raised her brows. "This is your idea of playing good client?"

He lifted his mug, his eyes laughing at her over the rim. "You didn't stipulate perfect. And I haven't really shown you bad yet."

She couldn't prevent the laugh. And when he joined her, she was charmed by the sound. "Okay. But you first."

He cupped his hands around his mug. "My parents were Susan and Darrell Stone. They met at a party my mother was waitressing at. He was a guest. It was love at first sight. Darrell Stone had some kind of secret government job that kept him away from home more than he was there."

As Jonah spoke, his tone was neutral. So were his eyes. Cilla felt her heart twist all the same.

"When I was a kid, the happiest days of my life were the ones he spent with us. He used to tell stories of the adventures he had, some in countries I'd never heard of. The year I was nine, he'd called my mom and promised to be home for Christmas. We waited and waited to open the presents and have dinner. But he never came, never sent word. Because of his work, my mother never had any way to contact him. Shortly after Christmas, the checks he always sent us stopped coming, and my mother went back to work waitressing. I watched her grow sadder and sadder. She kept telling me that he would come home soon, but I think it was to convince herself."

Jonah set down his mug, and Cilla reached out to take his hand in hers. The image of Jonah as a nine-year-old boy was so vivid in her mind.

"Six months after Christmas, a beautiful June day, my mom was struck and killed by a bus. Later, when I was older, I read the reports of the accident. Witnesses said she stepped in front of the bus. I don't think she could live without him."

"I am so sorry about your mother." Both parents had abandoned him and she couldn't begin to imagine what that might feel like. "Didn't anyone try to find your father?"

"Sure. A social worker told me they were doing their best to trace him, but no branch of the government employed a Darrell Stone who matched my father's description or age. So I went into foster care."

"Did *you* ever try to trace him? Gabe tells me you're the best hacker he's ever met."

"No. When I was young, I hadn't developed that skill yet." He shrugged. "By the time I did, I had no interest in finding my father. He'd been dead to me for a long time."

Cilla met his eyes steadily. "We'll have to try to locate him, see if he's still alive."

She waited a beat, and when he said nothing she continued, "We're already tracking down names of families and kids you met in foster care. Gabe is getting the names of people you came in contact with when you worked at the St. Francis Center."

"It's a long list, but you've already met one of the kids I knew in foster care. Virgil."

She glanced up at that.

"The first foster home I was in, he stood up for me. When I knew I was going to open Pleasures, I tracked him down. He was working in a bar over in Sausalito, and I hired him to manage my club."

"You hire Virgil from your first foster home, then

you hire Carmen from the St. Francis Center. You don't abandon your friends, Jonah Stone."

"I make good business decisions. Now it's your turn."

She set her pencil down. "My parents are Penny and Bradley Michaels. My mother has Boston blue blood in her veins, and my father met her when he was getting his MBA at Harvard. They divorced when I was five because my mother wanted more attention and he was focused totally on his work. He's had a stellar career and become a CEO at four Fortune 500 companies. He's currently trying to get a fifth one on the list. My mother's mission in life is to find Prince Charming. She's sure that husband number four, Bobby Laidlaw, is the one."

He studied her for a moment. She was giving him the same *Reader's Digest* version he'd given her. It only made him more curious. "How in hell did you end up becoming a cop?"

She smiled at him. "Textbook case of rebellion. My career still annoys my father. He calls me twice a year—on my birthday and at Christmas—and he always offers me a job with his current company."

"That's not the only reason you do the work you do."

"Maybe not. How did you end up creating places like Pleasures and Interludes?"

"I like creating worlds that offer people a chance to escape from the ordinary."

Her gaze didn't waver. "That's not the only reason. But—" she picked up her pencil "—we have other things to discuss."

Adjusting the pad so they both could read it, she wrote: *Christmases past, Interludes, Pleasures, for-*

tune, fleeting and *you're going to pay, six, five, four* and *counting.*

She tapped her pencil on *Christmases past.* "My hunch is we're going to find the answer here."

"I agree, but I'm coming up empty."

She moved her pencil to *six.* "That number has to mean something. What was going on at Christmas six years ago?"

He hadn't thought of that angle and he had to concentrate for a moment before it came to him. "I was still in Denver working for Gabe at G.W. Securities while I was getting together a business plan and attracting backers. Any spare time I had during the holiday season, I always helped out at the St. Francis Center."

"That would have been 2005. Can you think of anything more specific?"

Jonah frowned as the year suddenly rang a bell. "Yeah, now that you mention it. That was the year I spent Christmas here in San Francisco. This was where I wanted to open my first club because of St. Francis. I figured he'd always brought me good luck before, so I thought it was a good idea to begin in a city that was named after him. Nash's grandmother, Maggie Fortune, had gotten together a group of backers, and I asked her to come with me to look at some properties I had lined up."

"Was Carl Rockwell around? You said he was one of your original backers."

"No. I hadn't met any of them yet. It was just Nash's grandmother and me. Nash was overseas and I had some idea of getting her away from the Fortune Mansion over the holidays. We came up with the name of the club on that trip."

He smiled. "We spent every day for a week, save

Christmas Day, looking at real estate. And we found the building where Pleasures now stands."

"So that year, you were particularly focused on business."

"You could say that."

Cilla turned the pad around and began writing. "Gabe can check with Father Mike and contact Mrs. Fortune to see what they can remember about that December. In the meantime, we can't ignore other possibilities."

"But this is a good one. I can feel it." He placed a hand on hers. "You're good, Cilla Michaels."

"I need to get better." With her pencil, she tapped on the paper where he'd written *td*. "We need a better handle on who this Tank guy is. Part of what he's doing is carefully planned. The notes, the boxes and ribbon, even some of the places he chooses for delivery—it all needs to be precisely orchestrated."

She tapped her pencil again. "But there's a part of him that's less careful and more open to going with impulse. There's no way that he could have known we'd be at the police station this morning until we actually got there."

"You're right," Jonah mused. "And why would someone who has been so meticulous with this countdown-to-Christmas scenario hire a couple of low IQ thugs like Mickey P. and Lorenzo?"

"Or why drive a van that backfires? And last night at Pleasures, why lower the window and shoot his gun? Why not just drive away?"

"Temper? Maybe we're dealing with someone who isn't as stable as he thinks he is," Jonah said.

When her cell phone rang, she took the call. "Finelli, what have you got?" As she listened, she summarized the information for Jonah. "The bomb hadn't been fully wired yet. The bomb squad thinks we may have interrupted whoever was working on it." Then she went silent, listening hard.

When she finally disconnected Finelli's call, she looked straight at Jonah. "Someone on the bomb squad recognized the type of explosive. He'd served in the military and seen similar ones used in Iraq. Whoever built it was good, probably ex-military, and it would have had to be set off by a detonator. When Joe learned that, he had someone search the garage and they found the detonator in the stairwell on the floor where my car was parked."

Jonah thought for a moment. "The tracking device allowed Tank to locate your car and he was planting the bomb when we interrupted him. He slips away, and when he sees us checking the car, he panics and runs."

"And he tosses the detonator into a stairwell as he rounds the curve?" Cilla shook her head. "Why not take it with him?"

"Because his job was to plant the bomb. It was someone else's job to detonate it. I'm thinking Tank was working with someone who was standing in that stairwell waiting."

"A strong possibility." Then she shook her head again. "But there are still four nights and counting. Why would he blow you up today?"

Jonah reached for her hand and gripped it hard. "Not me. *You.* And with a detonator, he could have blown you up anytime."

"I would have found the bomb."

"That's what I've been telling myself. But if he was standing in that stairwell waiting, he could have detonated it while you were checking for the bomb." Fear snaked through him as he imagined what might have happened in the garage if they hadn't interrupted the driver of the van. Maybe he'd been wrong to insist that she personally handle his case. "Cilla…" he began.

"If you're thinking of firing me, forget it." Turning her hand, she linked her fingers with his. "You're the one who wanted a partner, and now you're stuck."

He was, Jonah realized as he gazed into those green eyes. He'd been stuck from the first. The thought tied an uneasy knot in his stomach. But the damage had been done. He wasn't going to be able to prevent himself from kissing her again, from having her again. And as he watched her eyes darken, he knew that she was coming to the same realization.

Cilla was the one who broke eye contact when Mark Gibbons arrived at their table and pulled out a chair. He placed four prints in front of Jonah. "Here's what we were able to get off the security discs."

The images were grainy, but the buzz-cut gray hair was clear. The man wore sunglasses, he had a square chin, and Jonah guessed him to be in his mid- to late fifties. He took his time, studying the prints one by one. Finally, he looked up and met Cilla's eyes. "I have no idea who this man is."

WHEN HE COULD THINK WITH SOME clarity again, the red mist was still a haze in front of his eyes. Blinking rapidly, he willed it away and focused on his surroundings. He was seated in his car, his fingers gripping the steering wheel.

The fire engine blocking off traffic at the corner told him that only a short time had passed. There were people standing on the street, huddled together for warmth in the chill winds. He'd heard the approaching sirens when he'd still been inside the garage. Bits and pieces of what had happened flashed into his mind in a series of quick-moving still photos.

He'd been standing in the stairwell watching through a narrow opening in the door when the plan he'd devised had been bungled again. His partner had promised no more failed missions, but he'd abandoned his assignment before he'd completed it. Then he'd panicked and driven off.

Again.

Just thinking about the backfiring van careening through the garage had his fury building again.

Stupid. Stupid. Stupid. Releasing his hold on the steering wheel, he beat his fists against it. Then reaching deep for control, he made himself breathe. And settle.

His partner was only partly to blame. That woman had interfered again. The bomb hadn't been fully engaged when she'd strode out of the elevator and headed toward her car. If it hadn't been for the clicking of her boots, his partner might have been discovered.

But he'd slithered out from under the car and crawled quietly along the wall in front of the other parked vehicles.

She'd come out too soon. Struggling again to control the anger, he gripped the steering wheel. If it hadn't been for her, he could have enjoyed the scenario he'd mapped out in his mind.

Closing his eyes, he replayed it. He would have been in the stairwell watching as she'd stepped out of the elevator. And he would have detonated the bomb then. It held a small blast, one that would have severely damaged her car and perhaps the adjacent vehicles. But it wouldn't have killed either Stone or the woman—not unless they were in the car.

It hadn't been his intent to kill Stone yet. Just as it hadn't been his intent to have him seriously hurt in the alley last night. But he would have had the pleasure of seeing Stone's face when the explosion occurred.

He would have seen fear on it this time. The man hadn't looked scared at all when he'd opened the green box in front of the police station this morning. He should be feeling the impact by now.

But Stone's face hadn't changed expression.

It was the woman's fault again. She was protecting him, making him feel safe by kicking guns out of people's hands, checking the cars.

It would have given him great satisfaction to see her face when her car exploded into smithereens.

He drew in another breath and let it out. He felt himself begin to calm. He still had time. Four more nights. Before this was over, he'd see fear on Jonah Stone's face.

There were all kinds of ways to create fear.

A smile curved his lips as the plan took form in his mind. It was the season for surprises.

9

INTERLUDES WAS NOT WHAT Cilla had expected. Her first surprise was the sign on the door that read Closed Until 4:00 p.m. on December 21 for a Private Party. The second surprise was the wall of noise that slapped into them the instant they stepped into the place.

The party was in full swing. And nearly everyone there was a kid. Out of habit, she moved slightly in front of Jonah. "I feel like I just stepped into munchkin land."

"Christmas party," Jonah explained.

"I can see that." The huge Christmas tree at the far end of the dining room with its multicolored blinking lights was a big clue. And blasting through the din of noise, "Jingle Bell Rock" poured through the sound system. She let her gaze take a quick sweep of the venue.

Two rooms opened off the large entrance area where they stood. Her image of a sports club had always contained lots of huge-screen TVs hanging from the ceiling, crowds drinking beer from big mugs and noise. Shouts, cheering, people doing happy dances and a lot of arm pumping.

Interludes provided all that. There were shouts of

"Hey, Jonah," when she and Jonah moved farther in. And the dining area to the left had the big flat-screened TVs all right. It also boasted a movie screen that nearly filled one wall.

The pint-size customers were drinking beer from big mugs. But since none of them looked to be over twelve, she guessed it was root beer, and most seemed more interested in a buffet spread that offered a seemingly endless variety of pizzas than they were in watching TV.

When she was able to drag her gaze away to meet Jonah's, he pitched his voice so she could hear it above the clamor. "Christmas party for all of the boys and girls clubs in the area. We throw them at other times of the year, but this is the big one."

It was big all right, she thought. At a rough estimate, she figured there were nearly a hundred children easy—just in the dining room. She looked around her. Small people in various shapes and sizes also filled the long room to her right. Only here, pool instead of food was the attraction. With its gleaming mahogany paneling and carved ceilings, the space reminded her of the game room of an expensive and exclusive men's club. Green shaded lamps hung over each of the more than a dozen pool tables. And here and there, adults helped the kids chalk cues and generally supervised the fun.

A woman stepped away from the nearest table and strode toward them. Cilla guessed her to be in her mid-forties. She wore a bright emerald colored silk shirt over slim black leggings, and her long, ash-blond hair was layered.

"Jonah, I was afraid you wouldn't make it." The rich voice with its genuine warmth and slightly Southern lilt had Cilla thinking briefly of the TV celebrity chef Paula Deen.

"Carmen, I'd like you to meet Cilla Michaels. She runs Gabe Wilder's office here in San Francisco." He turned to Cilla. "Carmen D'Annunzio runs Interludes even on a day like today when chaos is king."

Carmen laughed, and the sound was as rich and warm as her voice. "Long live chaos and Christmas. They make a perfect couple." Then she turned to Cilla and took one of her hands. "Welcome to Interludes."

"Jonah, come and play." A skinny boy with riotously curling dark hair shot over from one of the tables. "You promised that at this party you'd clear the tables again."

"Rack the balls," Jonah said, stripping off his jacket as he followed the boy.

One of the other boys raced into the bar and whistled for silence. When the din lowered a few decibels, he said, "Jonah's going to hit all the balls into the pockets. C'mon."

Carmen put two fingers into her mouth and did her own whistle to prevent the stampede. Raising both hands, she said, "Hold on. I'll get it on the TV screens."

"C'mon," she said to Cilla as she moved quickly to a console in a corner of the dining room and punched a few buttons. Suddenly all the screens showed Jonah bending over the pool table. Cilla stared fascinated at the large movie screen as he made his first shot. Three balls disappeared into pockets.

"He's good," she murmured.

"Never seen anyone better," Carmen said. "We've been open four years now, and he puts on this show a couple of times a year. Closes down the place for the afternoon and lets the kids party. How about a root beer? I've also got lemonade and more traditional colas. I'm only serving the soft stuff this afternoon."

"I'd love a root beer." Cilla climbed onto a stool

at a raised table while Carmen filled two glasses and joined her.

The din in the room had quieted a bit as the kids grabbed more food and settled into seats to watch the show. Jonah's next shot ricocheted off two others balls and sent them into different pockets.

Cilla positioned her seat so that she had a good view of the pool room. She watched as David Santos slipped through the front door. Mark Gibbons was with him. She signaled Santos into the room with Jonah and Mark slipped behind the hostess desk. They'd arrived in three separate taxis she'd had Mark call before they'd left Janine's.

Catching Carmen watching her, she said, "Two of my men."

"I know David Santos. He's a regular customer here."

Cilla glanced back up at the nearest TV screen. Jonah was walking around the table considering his next shot. He looked so relaxed that his only care in the world might have been to sink another ball. It was as if he'd shed the first part of the day including the bomb scare as easily as he'd shed his jacket.

If he had, she envied him. More, she needed to emulate him. Thinking about the might-have-beens would only distract her from thinking about the what-might-bes. Using taxis for transportation could work for a while. But the bastard who wanted to hurt Jonah would have a backup plan, too.

She turned her gaze to Carmen. "I need a quiet place to make a quick phone call."

Carmen pointed to a door at the far end of the room. "My office."

Cilla left the door open as she punched a number into

her cell. From her position, she could see Jonah on the screens. A more direct view of him was blocked by the kids who'd moved closer to his pool table.

"Hello, my favorite cop."

"Not a cop anymore, T.D." Five years ago, T.D. short for Top Dog, had been her first snitch when she'd been a beat cop. He'd given her two of her first collars, and she'd arranged for him to get a legitimate job as a limo driver. Last time she'd talked to him he was well on his way to an associate's degree at a local community college, and then he'd married his boss's daughter.

A laugh boomed into her ear. "And I'm not your snitch. Instead, I'm driving around San Francisco in a honey of a limo."

"I want to hire you later today. Can you do it?"

"For you, sugar, I'll rearrange my schedule. When and where?"

"I need a pickup at least four or five blocks away from the St. Francis Hotel between 5:30 and 6:30. My client has a late-afternoon meeting there. Someone may try to tail us from the hotel, so I'll shake them and then come to you."

"You got it. When you're ready, give me a call and I'll give you my specific location. Bye, sugar."

After disconnecting, Cilla punched in Gabe's number. When he picked up immediately, she filled him in on the day's events and the fact that both she and Jonah had a feeling about the Christmas of 2005. "Was Mark Gibbons working for you then?" she asked.

"He started that fall. You want me to check him out."

It wasn't a question. Still, she waited a beat. "I do. Do you think I'm being paranoid?"

"No. One of the reasons I hired you, Cilla, is because we think alike. I'm already checking Gibbons and Santos out. Santos is from Denver and he was in the Marines until two years ago. He worked with explosives, and some of his records are classified. But I can't find a connection between either of them and Jonah. Yet. Anyone else you want me to check into?"

"Yes. The backers that Mrs. Fortune put together for Pleasures. The deal was coming together that year."

"So it was. I hadn't thought of that angle."

"One of his current partners, Carl Rockwell, was also one of the backers for Pleasures."

"Got it. Call me if you want anything else. And, Cilla?"

"Yes?"

"Don't let him get hurt."

A deafening roar of applause and cheers had Cilla glancing up at the big screen again. She'd missed the shot, but the children were jumping up and down around Jonah's table.

When she returned to her seat at the bar, the kids had quieted, their eyes glued on Jonah.

His back was to her, larger than life on the screen. Though she knew she should, she didn't look away. Instead, she let her system absorb the way his black wool turtleneck fit over the broad shoulders like a second skin. The burning sensation in her hands reminded her of how hard those shoulder muscles had felt beneath her palms. Her pulse skipped as she let her gaze drift down the lean back to the narrow waist, the tight, hard butt and those long legs. Her throat went dry as dust.

It had been nearly a month since that body had been hers to touch, to explore at whim. And she hadn't been able to stop thinking about touching him again. Not during those long lonely nights and certainly not since he'd walked toward her in the airport garage yesterday.

The kisses they'd exchanged had only deepened her hunger.

She had to touch him again. Slowly, thoroughly. She needed to feel his naked skin heat, then tremble. She wanted to once more hear her name on his lips. Desire burned in her belly and simmered in her blood. She wasn't even looking directly at him, just at his image on a screen, and yet the pull, the attack on her senses, were as intense as if she had been standing directly behind him in the room.

And if she *had* been standing behind him? Would she have been able to resist putting her hands on him? She drew in a breath and felt the burn in her lungs. She thought of all those nights she'd spent without him. Long silent nights filled with nothing but sexy fantasies of touching Jonah, tasting him, feeling him thrusting inside of her again. And again.

She didn't want the fantasy anymore. She wanted the real thing. Longing spread through every pore of her being, and she had to grip the edge of the table hard to keep herself from going to him. No man had ever triggered this kind of response in her, this kind of greed. She might talk a good game about ground rules, but it wasn't to Jonah that she had to pitch her argument. It was to herself.

When she reached for her root beer, she was stunned to realize that her hand was trembling. She fisted it on the tabletop and looked back at the screen.

"A lot of eye candy there," Carmen murmured. "The girls all have a crush on him, the boys all want to *be* him."

Cilla blinked, then dragged her eyes away from the image of Jonah. *Job,* she reminded herself. "What about the grown-ups who are here? How do they feel about Jonah?"

"Probably a mix of admiration and envy."

"Do you know all of them?"

"Met a few of them for the first time today. They're parents or volunteers and workers at the various clubs."

"Any of them come alone?"

"No. They all came with groups of kids."

Cilla glanced back at the pool room and saw that Santos had chosen a space within a few feet of Jonah.

"Virgil told me what happened at Pleasures last night," Carmen said. "He was nearly mugged. But that's not all of it, is it? There's more."

For a moment, Cilla didn't speak. Jonah trusted Carmen and Virgil, but she couldn't discount the fact that someone close to him, probably someone from his past, had a hand in the threats.

But her gut told her that Carmen wasn't that person. And Jonah's gut was telling him the same thing. Going with those feelings, she outlined what had happened.

"Well, shit." Carmen set her root beer down with enough force that it sloshed over the rim of the glass. "This is his favorite time of year. And to me, he embodies the true spirit of Christmas. Jonah loves throwing the parties. Not just this one. The shindig he has going on at Pleasures tomorrow night—all the movers and shakers in the city will be there. Over the years, he's built it into *the* event of the season, and the money he collects goes to the boys and girls clubs." She swept a hand around. "Eventually to these kids."

"Do you have any idea who might be sending the notes?"

"No." She met Cilla's eyes. "Tell me what I can do to help."

BUSINESS REPLY MAIL
FIRST-CLASS MAIL   PERMIT NO. 717   BUFFALO, NY

POSTAGE WILL BE PAID BY ADDRESSEE

THE READER SERVICE
PO BOX 1867
BUFFALO NY 14240-9952

NO POSTAGE
NECESSARY
IF MAILED
IN THE
UNITED STATES

Send For
2 FREE BOOKS
Today!

I accept your offer!

Please send me two free
Harlequin® Blaze® novels and
two mystery gifts (gifts worth
about $10). I understand that
these books are completely
free—even the shipping and
handling will be paid—and I am
under no obligation to purchase
anything, ever, as explained on the
back of this card.

151/351 HDL FH9S

Please Print

FIRST NAME

LAST NAME

ADDRESS

APT.#   CITY

STATE/PROV.   ZIP/POSTAL CODE

Visit us online at
www.ReaderService.com

"You can start by answering some questions."

"Go ahead."

"Jonah told me that you used to volunteer at the St. Francis Center for Boys in Denver. How well did you know him?"

"I knew him mostly through my sons. He's wonderful with kids. When my husband died ten years ago, my boys were ten and twelve. They were a handful even then. The only job I could get was bartending. I hired someone to come in at night, but I needed a place for my boys to go after school and on weekends. The St. Francis Center was perfect."

Cilla couldn't help but think how closely Carmen's story echoed Jonah's and his mother's experience. Except that Jonah had lost his mother as well as his father. Both of his parents had abandoned him. But Jonah didn't abandon people. "Were you surprised when he asked you to move here and manage Interludes?"

"I was stunned." Carmen met her eyes, and Cilla saw a glint of tears. "It meant I had to uproot the kids, but they were older, close to making me an empty nester. And Jonah made everything so easy for me. It's the best decision I ever made."

The skinny kid with the mop of curls came racing up to Carmen at the bar. "Jonah needs fuel."

Carmen's brows shot up. "Well, load a plate up for him. We can't have the boss going hungry."

"Yes, ma'am." The boy shot off to the buffet.

"This is a very different place than Pleasures," Cilla commented.

"Well, you're seeing us on a special day. But if I were to use some of that fancy business school mumbo jumbo that my oldest son, Jack, uses, I'd say that the mission statements of the two clubs are the same. Basically, Jonah's goal is to create places for people to shed their cares and worries for a short time. Places that they can enter into for a while and just play. And people have different price points and different images of their escape spaces."

"Fantasy worlds," Cilla murmured.

"You could call them that. But for a short time, they're reality. It's not a whole lot different from what Father Mike did when he started the St. Francis Center. He created a safe space for kids to play and learn and grow, a place that sheltered them and helped them deal better with the reality outside."

"It's like what a home should do," Cilla commented.

"Yeah," Carmen agreed. "When everything's ideal. But that can be a hard thing to pull off. I know."

Cilla thought of her own home—her father working, her mother unhappy. She might not have liked it; her mother certainly hadn't. But it had been there. Her parents, as imperfect as they might be, were still there.

She glanced up at the big screen again and saw that Jonah had set his pool stick aside to eat the pizza the skinny boy had brought him. As she watched, the kid burst into laughter and Jonah joined him. She felt her heart take a tumble. He looked so right standing there.

He claimed that he'd created these clubs to provide customers with an escape, but she wondered if he hadn't really built them as a way of establishing a home for himself.

And she was letting him distract her again. Turning to Carmen, she said, "You were volunteering at the St. Francis Center six years ago, right? That would have been Christmastime, 2005."

"Sure. My boys were still in high school—sixteen

and fourteen. Tough ages. I was there when I could be. Why?"

"I want you to think about that year at Christmastime. Jonah wasn't in Denver. He was here in San Francisco checking out possible places for Pleasures."

She frowned, thinking. "What happens at my age is that the years begin to blur."

"That year, 2005, might be important. Think about it." She passed a card to Carmen. "And let me know."

Carmen met her eyes. "I'll do more than think about it, I'll ask my sons. The younger one will have pictures. Father Mike got him his first camera, put him in charge of making a pictorial history of the center. Ben fell in love with photography. That's his major in college, and he kept pictures that he took at the center. What are we looking for?"

Cilla shook her head. "I wish I knew. The notes he's receiving are telling him he has to pay for something. And they mention Christmases past."

"The Dickens's *Christmas Carol* thing," Carmen murmured.

"If you can remember anyone he offended that year. Any feathers that got ruffled around the center. Maybe somebody took it wrong that he went off to San Francisco on business." Cilla remembered the Christmases that her father had been away on business and how much she'd resented it.

"I'll have Ben find the photos," Carmen said.

A cheer went up from the kids in the bar. Cilla glanced up at the screen to see that Jonah's pool table was clear of balls except for the cue ball. "He is really good."

"Yeah." Carmen put a hand over hers. "Jonah's like

a kid brother to me. Virgil feels the same way. And he says that Jonah's more than a case to you."

"Yes." No use denying it. A man with Virgil's eagle eye hadn't missed their kiss in the bar last night. And she'd spent most of her time here staring at Jonah on the big screen like a teenager.

Carmen's gaze turned assessing and some of the warmth faded. "You're not his type."

She lifted her chin. "I don't want to be his type. I didn't want him to be more than a case to me."

The warmth returned to Carmen's eyes and her lips curved into a smile. "Sometimes it happens that way. Just don't let him get hurt."

Carmen was the third person who'd said those words to her in just that tone. Jonah seemed to have quite a loyal following, and that didn't surprise her. He wasn't the career-minded businessman she'd first thought him to be.

Over Carmen's shoulder, she watched him striding toward her, one arm around the skinny kid, the other around a chubby redheaded girl with freckles. When she met his eyes, absorbed the smile, something moved through her. Even though her toes curled, it wasn't merely the pull she always felt. Or the fire in her belly she was almost getting used to. What she felt was that warmer, softer feeling she'd experienced when he'd kissed her so tenderly in the garage. As it spread, she all but heard a click inside her as something unlocked.

She pressed a hand to her stomach as fear bubbled up brightly. How had it come to this? How had she fallen in love with him?

And those weren't questions she could afford to think about now. She had to focus on keeping him safe. Her gut told her that the clock was ticking on that one.

IT WAS NEARLY FOUR BEFORE Jonah hung his pool stick on the rack and watched the last of the kids reluctantly exit through the front door of Interludes. There was a part of him that looked forward to this party every year. But he was also aware there was a part of him that had wanted very much for the party to end.

And that was because of Cilla.

Usually, he could completely lose himself in a game of pool. Playing allowed him to clear his mind for a while. Today, there hadn't been one moment when he'd been able to totally focus on the position of the balls or to imagine the possible angles for a shot.

Because she'd been watching him. Sometimes, he would look up and catch her doing just that. Other times he was pretty sure he'd felt her watching him on the TV screens.

How in the hell was that possible? He ran a hand through his hair.

He studied her now as she paced in the dining room, the phone pressed to her ear. She was in Priscilla mode, jotting down notes, figuring the angles.

But there was that moment earlier when he'd walked into the dining room and his eyes had met hers—she'd been Cilla then. Something in her look had slammed into him like a Mack truck, triggering so many emotions, so many needs.

He'd been outrageously tempted to just go to her, grab her off that stool, and carry her off somewhere. Only the fact that he'd been surrounded by kids and someone was trying to kill her had stopped him. Caveman tactics had never been his style, but as he watched her pace, he was beginning to see their value.

It had been hours since he'd touched her, kissed her. It might as well have been years. And it was going to be far too long until he could get her back to Pleasures and into his bed.

A quick glance at his watch told him that they were due at the St. Francis Hotel in half an hour. And he'd never been more tempted in his life to blow off a business meeting. Carl would understand. But Stanley Rubin had called the meeting as a favor. Jonah couldn't let him down.

One thing he was sure of, the two quick kisses he'd stolen during the endless day hadn't been enough. But they'd certainly tapped out his self-control. He'd better keep his distance and play by her ground rules until they were safely in his apartment.

Pushing himself away from the pool table, he strode into the entrance hall.

"I'll lock the door," Mark Gibbons said.

Jonah turned to the man, who hadn't left his post at the hostess desk all afternoon. Carmen had brought him a plate of food at one point, but he'd remained where he could check out anyone who came through the door.

"Boss wants to have a brief meeting before we leave for your business appointment at the hotel," Gibbons said.

Turning, Jonah saw that Cilla now sat at a table with Santos, out of the way of the waitstaff that was whisking away the debris of the party.

Jonah turned to Gibbons. "I have a couple of questions for you. Why did you leave the Denver office?"

"Gabe asked me to come here temporarily." Gibbons studied him for a moment. "If you're wondering if I wanted her job, if I'm carrying some kind of grudge because Gabe put her in charge of the office instead of me, I'm not. And I didn't plant a bomb under her car."

"Why didn't you want the job?"

"Because I've got a girlfriend back in Denver who is not happy about the situation. I go back there on my weekends off. She comes here on the others. If I took a permanent job here, she'd send me packing."

"So Gabe asked you to play what—big brother-slash-mentor until Cilla is comfortable?"

"Gabe is less concerned about her than the rest of the staff. Santos is new, both to the business and to G.W. He's great with the electronic security. He got some training in the military and then he worked for a casino in Vegas. I've been training him in the personal security side. Cilla's only new to G.W., but she's smart, she has good contacts here in the police department. Plus, her political instincts are good. Her instincts are good, period. She's got a mind that's always figuring the angles."

"Do you know why she left her personal security job in L.A.?"

"Sure. She told all of us at our first staff meeting. One of the teen idols she'd been assigned to got a little high and made some advances. She defended herself and as a result the production on his movie was delayed. The producers made a stink."

"But you dug a little deeper than that," Jonah guessed.

"Sure." His expression turned grim. "According to my sources, the guy tried to rape her. She knocked two of his teeth out and gave him a black eye. No charges were filed, but pretty boy couldn't film for nearly a week and the firm she worked for was being pressured to fire her. She quit first."

As Jonah studied Cilla, anger mixed with admiration. "She's one tough cookie."

"I'd say so." Mark patted him on the shoulder. "And in one more minute she's going to come over here and read us the riot act because we're delaying her strategy meeting. I'd like to keep my teeth."

"Me, too." Jonah walked with Mark to join her.

10

A HALF HOUR LATER, CILLA stepped out of a taxi in front of the St. Francis Hotel. After a quick scan of the area, she signaled Jonah to follow her. The late-afternoon sun was low in the sky and the air was cold and crisp.

The plan had been to take three taxis again—she and Jonah in the first, David Santos in a second and Mark Gibbons in the third. Out of the corner of her eye, she noted David's taxi had stopped across the street. He was already mixing into passengers disembarking from a cable car.

Pedestrians loaded down with packages milled along the sidewalk in front of the hotel. She steered Jonah through them. She hadn't spotted a tail, but if someone had followed them, they'd have to deal with the parking issue. She and Jonah wouldn't.

They were halfway up the steps when Mark strode past them and into the hotel. The lobby was aglow with Christmas. Tired shoppers with packages stacked on the floor had filled the bar to overflowing. Above the laughter and conversation, she caught the sounds of a string quartet playing "White Christmas."

They moved toward the elevators where Mark

was already waiting for a car. Everything was going smoothly. The ride over had been short. And Jonah had played the role of good client perfectly. He hadn't touched her. She'd been so sure that he would kiss her. An afternoon of watching him on the big screen and not being able to touch him had been nearly as frustrating as the three-and-a-half weeks she'd spent avoiding her bed because he wasn't in it.

By the time she'd decided that she should play bad security agent, the taxi had stopped in front of the St. Francis.

On the bright side, she'd been able to fill him in on what she'd discussed with Carmen. He'd filled her in on the Rubins.

One of the elevator doors opened. Quickly, she moved into the car with Jonah, then shifted so that she stood in front of him as she scanned the lobby. Mark followed a crowd of shoppers into the same car. She spotted David Santos leaning against one of the walls, reading a newspaper as the elevator doors closed. His job was to keep watch in the lobby. If there was any sign of the driver of the backfiring van, he would notify them.

Everything was going smoothly, like clockwork. And it wasn't disappointment she was feeling because Jonah had finally decided to stick to her ground rules. She should be worrying about why she had an itchy sensation at the back of her neck. There was no reason for it—unless it was connected to the sexual frustration she was feeling.

Focus, she told herself. As the elevator crept slowly upward, she reviewed the information Jonah had given her on Stanley Rubin, who'd amassed a fortune building condos and upscale apartment complexes in San Diego.

Just as he'd promised, Jonah had notified Stan that he was bringing a personal security agent with him because of the attempted mugging last night. According to Jonah, Stan's reaction had been concern and then approval that Jonah was taking precautions.

Joining Stan and Carl at the meeting would be Rubin's wife, Glenda, and his young associate, Dean Norris. When she'd asked Jonah who had initiated the meeting, he'd said, "Stan. We're due to start renovating the property for our new club right after the first of the year. Norris has some new design ideas that Stan wants Carl and me to see. My understanding is that they conflict with the vision I originally presented them for the club. Both he and Glenda are coming to the party at Pleasures tomorrow evening. And since Stan loves to mix business with pleasure—his words—he asked for a meeting."

"And what about this Dean Norris?" she'd asked. "What do you know about him?"

"Norris joined Rubin Enterprises a year ago when he left the army. Stan believes he's got a bright future with the company."

When they finally reached the top floor, Mark stepped out of the elevator ahead of them and led the way down the hall. He'd keep watch on the door to the Rubins' suite until they left.

But as they approached the suite, Cilla felt the itchy feeling at the back of her neck intensify. Turning, she glanced back down the hallway.

Empty except for a woman in a cap and down jacket inserting her key into a lock.

"You can relax." Jonah spoke softly as they reached

the door. "Gabe vetted Stan thoroughly. I don't go into business with anyone I have questions about. You're going to like him."

Like him or not, Cilla glanced down the hall in the other direction as they waited. But she spotted no one other than Mark, and he was turning a corner to check out the rest of the floor. For a moment the hall was empty.

But the itchy feeling remained. Maybe it *was* due to sexual frustration. When Jonah raised his hand to knock, she grabbed his wrist.

"What's wrong?" He gave the hallway a quick scan.

"You didn't kiss me in the taxi."

She saw surprise in the look he gave her, but it didn't come close to matching her own surprise at what she'd said. Then she saw the heat and the hint of recklessness flash into his eyes, and her bones began to melt.

"I've just spent a whole afternoon wanting you and not being able to so much as touch you. If I'd kissed you in the taxi, I wouldn't have stopped with a kiss." He picked up a piece of her hair and twisted it around his finger. "Have you ever made love in the backseat of a taxi?"

"No." But she had a quick flash of what it might be like with Jonah, and she couldn't feel her legs anymore. Leaning against the door of the Rubins' suite didn't help one bit. Because then all she could think of was the door in that hotel room and what he'd done to her. What she very much wanted him to do again.

"I decided that I wanted a little more space and some privacy the next time we make love." He released her hair to run a finger slowly over her lips. "The next time I kiss you, I'm not going to stop until I'm inside you making you come."

Everything inside of her clenched at the image. For a moment, she thought she might come right then.

Jonah tore his gaze away from her and knocked on the door. Glenda Rubin answered the summons almost immediately. If she hadn't, Jonah wasn't quite sure he could have kept from taking Cilla right there in the hallway.

And if he had? Well, he'd spoken nothing less than the truth about the reason he'd kept his hands to himself in the taxi. But saying the words out loud had badly weakened his self-control. And it hadn't been in good shape on the ride over. Each time the cab took a corner and her shoulder brushed against his, he'd nearly been a goner.

A hallway provided more space and at least the possibility of greater privacy than the backseat of a taxi with hundreds of pedestrians out Christmas shopping. But he wanted more than that the next time he touched Cilla.

And he intended to touch her soon.

Glenda enveloped him in a hug. "Merry Christmas. Carl's already here and Dean is on his way." She grasped Cilla's hand when Jonah made the introductions. "Welcome."

The suite she led them into was large and airy. Windows along one wall offered a stunning view of the Golden Gate Bridge, where the late-afternoon sun was moving closer to the horizon.

Carl Rockwell and Stan Rubin already stood near the conference table. The sight of them helped Cilla snap back into security agent mode. But she was very careful not to look at Jonah.

Stan was a tall man with white hair and a neatly trimmed beard and mustache. His eyes were blue, his smile warm, and if he'd been portly instead of slim, Cilla decided that he would have reminded her of Santa Claus. Carl Rockwell looked as fit and dapper as he had when she'd met him in the bar at Pleasures.

Cilla liked Glenda, too. The woman was nearly as tall as her husband. She wore her blond hair pulled back in a classic chignon and looked quietly elegant in a champagne-colored sweater and slacks.

The Rubins looked to be in their late fifties, just about the same age as Carl. All three expressed genuine concern about the attempted mugging. Carl had evidently given them a blow-by-blow description already. Glenda took Jonah's hand in both of hers. "How troubling. This should be a season filled with joy."

"You're smart to hire protection," Stan said.

"And G.W. Securities is where you started out, isn't it?" Carl asked. "I admire loyalty."

Jonah glanced at Cilla. "And I like hiring the best."

Stan smiled. "Always the smart move. Dean will be joining us in a minute, but before he does, Glenda and I have been thinking of investing in this winery in Napa, and I'd like your opinion about this Cabernet I picked up. You, too, Carl."

As the men moved toward the conference table, Glenda took her arm. "I asked room service to send up some canapés. Would you mind helping me with them?"

Cilla followed Glenda to a small kitchenette and watched her remove a bottle of white wine from the refrigerator. She could use a little break from being elbow to elbow with Jonah.

At the other end of the large suite, still in plain sight, she could see Stan Rubin uncork a bottle of red wine and fill three glasses. But she couldn't hear what the men were saying. The young man who joined them wore dark-framed glasses. He had a slender build with straight dark hair that fell over his forehead. He carried a laptop computer.

Dean Norris, she surmised. He had a military bearing and precise movements, which matched the brief résumé Jonah had given her. He had to have joined the army at a young age because she judged him to still be in his mid-twenties.

"I'm sorry about sweeping you away like this," Glenda said. "It's so women-in-the-kitchen, men-doing-the-important-business." She wrinkled her nose. "But because I love Stan and know him, I've schooled myself to think of it in other terms. Stan spent a few years in the Air Force. You should have seen him in uniform. I tell myself that he wants me to play the role of wingman. Are you familiar with the term?"

"Sure. As a bodyguard, that's my role with Jonah."

"And he's right there where you can see him," Glenda pointed out as she uncorked the bottle.

"But Stan wants a private meeting with Dean, Carl and Jonah," Cilla said.

"Exactly." Glenda poured wine into two glasses. "Stan favors the reds, but I love the whites. I know they're not as fashionable. But this one is really good. Would you like a taste? I know you're on duty."

"I can probably handle a taste."

Glenda beamed a smile at her. "I knew I liked you. Sometimes it happens that way. You just feel it." She glanced over at the men as she handed Cilla a glass. "The meeting is about Dean. Stan believes he has a lot of promise and he wants to encourage him."

Cilla said nothing as Glenda pulled out some trays from the small refrigerator. "Dean has some design ideas that would change the theme of the club we're opening in San Diego. Stan doesn't agree with them, but he wants Dean to run them by Jonah and Carl so that he'll feel his ideas are being given serious consideration."

"And Stan gets some backup for rejecting them."

"Exactly."

"What kind of theme change does Dean want to make?"

"Have you been to any of Jonah's clubs?" Glenda asked.

"I've been to Pleasures and I just spent over two hours at Interludes. Pleasures takes you back in time to a gilded age. I'm not sure I got the full theme of Interludes because there were about two hundred kids romping through the rooms."

Glenda laughed. "You were at the Christmas party he throws every year for various youth organizations. Stan and I visited the Easter Party he gave for them last spring before we decided to propose this new club."

"Did you watch him shoot pool with the kids?"

"Yes. The way the kids looked at him—that was the clincher for me. I knew we should do business with him. Stan bought in when Jonah showed them how to clear the table. His work with young people is what inspired Stan to take on Dean Norris as a special assistant on this project. Dean was the one who suggested Stan look into the idea of opening a club in the first place. He even suggested he contact Jonah. He's such a hard worker and he wants so badly to impress Jonah."

Cilla glanced across the length of the suite and saw that Dean had set up his laptop on the conference table. A screen had been lowered on the wall, and the young man was hooking his computer up to a projector.

"How did you meet Dean?"

"About a year ago, he showed up at Stan's office one day and asked for work. He said he wanted to learn the business from the bottom up. He'd take any job. It was exactly the right approach to take with Stan. He's a self-made man. He wasn't born with blue blood or a silver spoon in his mouth, and he made it to where he is on his own. Jonah, too. That's one of the things Stan likes about Jonah."

"And Stan saw that same possibility in Dean."

"Yes."

For the first time, Cilla saw the hint of a frown in Glenda's eyes. "You're worried about this meeting."

"Dean doesn't always take criticism or rejection easily, and since he feels it was his idea, this club in San Diego is very special to him. He's very enthused about his designs. You'll be able to see them on the screen."

Cilla watched the sketches flash onto the large panel. The drawings reminded her a bit of what she'd seen at Pleasures, the feeling of an elegant world in the past.

"What do you think?" Glenda asked as she took a sip of her own wine.

"They remind me of Pleasures."

Glenda let out a soft sigh. "That's what Stan thinks, too. Jonah's designs for this club are much more modern, more edgy. They're calling it Inclinations, and the idea will be to attract young people."

When the screen went dark, Stan hit a wall switch to enhance the light and handed Dean a glass of wine. Glenda picked up her tray and moved across the room. With her own glass in hand, Cilla followed.

"Your designs are impressive, Dean," Jonah was saying. "Hold on to them. They might work very well in a club I'm thinking of opening farther up the coast in Seattle."

"I'd appreciate that, sir."

"Jonah."

Dean nodded. "After my years in the service, it's hard to break the habit." He turned to Carl. "What did you think, sir?"

Carl smiled at him. "I have to agree with Jonah. Your designs show real promise, but I think we have to go with Jonah's concept for the San Diego club."

Stan placed a hand on Dean's shoulder. "It's got to be a disappointment, but I have to agree with Jonah and Carl. Sticking with our original concept is the way to go."

"It's your call, sir. I appreciate your giving me the chance to show you my ideas."

"Time for refreshments." Glenda moved around the conference table and offered the canapés. Stan topped off Carl's and Jonah's glasses and turned the conversation to the wine.

When the doorbell of the suite rang, Glenda set the food down and frowned. "That can't be my sister Barbara. I told her six."

Stan glanced at his watch and sighed. "Barbara is always early. And if she and Hank have been in San Francisco shopping with that clan of theirs, I'm figuring they both are in need of a large glass of this red."

Cilla felt her cell vibrate. Moving closer to the balcony doors, she saw that it was a text from Mark Gibbons. "Thirteen people in front of the suite. Eight adults, three young boys, two teenagers."

As she thumbed in an acknowledgment, the sound of voices and laughter floated in from the foyer. Above it, she heard Stan say, "I know you have plans, Carl, but,

Jonah, you and Cilla are welcome to stay for dinner if you want. Barbara and Hank's three grandchildren are what I kindly refer to as a 'handful.' That's why we ordered room service instead of taking them out to a restaurant."

"Thanks," Jonah said. "But I'll want to check in at Pleasures."

"Figured. Big night tomorrow. Glenda and I are looking forward to it. We'll see you there, Carl?"

"Wouldn't miss it."

A burst of laughter shifted Cilla's attention to the foyer area, where Glenda was receiving hugs from three small boys.

"We haven't been formally introduced."

Cilla turned to see that Dean Norris had joined her at the balcony windows. He had a smile on his face, the first one she'd seen since he'd entered the suite earlier. And there was none of the stiffness she'd heard in his tone when he'd been fielding the bad news from Jonah and the others.

"I'm Dean Norris and I work for Stan."

She took his outstretched hand. "Cilla Michaels. I work for Jonah."

"He's a very lucky man. I envy him. Stan mentioned that someone tried to mug him outside his club last night. That's got to be hard, especially during the Christmas season. But the upside is that he gets to have a beautiful bodyguard."

Cilla was saved from having to make a reply when three little boys, the ones who'd been hugging Glenda, exploded into the room and shot straight toward the balcony doors.

"Watch out." Dean took her arm and drew her away from the stampede just in time to avoid a collision.

"Look, the sun's a ginormous red ball and it's setting," one of them shouted.

"It's going to hit the Golden Gate Bridge on the way down and 'splode!" the second boy said.

"Nah," the third one argued. "It'll just sink into the water."

"You're wrong, too," the first one insisted. "The sun isn't sinking. The earth is rotating. Simple third-grade science."

Cilla heard Stan mutter to Jonah. "A handful. The one with the stellar science knowledge is my namesake, Stan."

Carl set his glass down and patted the older Stan on the shoulder. "Enjoy them. I'll see you both tomorrow at Pleasures. Take care, Jonah."

"Enjoy them," Dean spoke in an impatient undertone to Cilla. "Someone ought to control them. I only wish I had Stone's or Rockwell's excuse for leaving."

As other guests filtered in, Cilla kept her gaze on Dean. Seconds ago, he'd been affable, almost charming. Now tension radiated from every pore in his body. "Can't you just say that you want to work on your designs and sneak off to your room?"

Anger flashed into his eyes. "I'll have to say that I'm working on some new ones since the ones I brought today were a total failure. Stone's a tough man to compete with, especially since he's got the money to make sure his designs win."

"But Glenda says that you were the one who urged Stan to open a club. If it's successful, he's going to give you the credit for that."

"And if it fails, I'm sure I'll get the credit for that also. Stone will still come out on top. That's what he's always done. It's…frustrating."

The words had come out in a rush and it wasn't just anger she heard now, but passion. "You believe that your designs are truly better than Jonah's?"

"I know they are. I just need a chance to prove it."

"Then take Jonah up on his offer. Talk to him about the club he's thinking of opening in Seattle."

Dean's eyes narrowed. "He just said that to make me feel better."

She reached out and laid a hand on his arm. "No. He's not a man who lies to people he does business with."

Whatever Dean might have responded was prevented by Glenda's approach. She had her arm linked with a woman who might have been her twin.

"Cilla, I want to introduce you to my sister Barbara and her husband, Hank."

She'd barely acknowledged the introductions before her cell rang. "Pardon me," she murmured to Glenda, then stepped away to take the call.

"Santos," the voice said. "I just spotted our guy Tank in the hotel."

"You're sure?" Cilla asked.

"Not at first. He was wearing a baseball cap, and I might have missed him if he hadn't raised his voice to the bell captain. I circled around to get a better look at him, and the instant he spotted me, he took off. By the time I got out to the street, he'd vanished. And there's more."

Cilla felt the back of her neck begin to itch again. "What?"

"I'm talking to the bell captain right now. He says the guy tipped him to deliver a gift bag to Room 820."

"That's Stanley Rubin's suite."

"Bingo. I tipped the captain again and told him I'd

deliver the bag. It contains a little green box tied with a red ribbon."

"Stay there, but let Gibbons know what's going on. I'll come to get the bag. Call me if you spot Tank again." Then she turned to signal Jonah.

THE INSTANT CILLA FILLED him in on the delivery of a new gift bag, Jonah took her arm and steered her toward the door of the suite. As he nodded and smiled to Stan and Glenda's relatives, questions swirled in his mind, each one increasing his sense of urgency. Why had another green box been delivered? The bastard had already sent him one today. Did that mean he was moving up the timetable? And how had the man known Stan's room number? Hotels were pretty careful not to give out that information.

Anger sparked to life inside him, and he leashed it down hard. It wouldn't do him any good. Hadn't he learned that lesson years ago from Father Mike? He could almost hear the priest's voice in his ear telling him that anger never solved anything. You had to push it aside or it could blind you to everything life held in store.

But he wanted Cilla out of the hotel and back at Pleasures. She would be safe there. And he wanted to spend time with her. Not just to make love with her—although he wanted that, too. But they needed to talk. Maybe together, they could make some sense of what was happening and put an end to it.

Finally, only Glenda and a room service cart stood between them and the door of the suite. She pushed the cart out of the way and gave Cilla a hug. "I'm so glad to have met you." Then she took Jonah's hand and gave it a squeeze. "Thanks so much for letting Dean down easy. Stan and I won't forget it."

Jonah smiled at her. "Tell him I meant what I told him. I think his idea might work for a place I'm thinking about in Seattle."

Glenda leaned in and kissed his cheek. "You're a charming man, Jonah Stone. We'll see you both tomorrow night."

She opened the door, then said, "Wait." Turning, she took a gift bag from a small table and handed it to Jonah. "I left this here so I wouldn't forget it. But I nearly did."

"A gift?" Jonah asked. "You shouldn't have."

"I didn't. The man who delivered the room service cart gave it to me. He said that someone handed it to him while he was loading carts into the elevator and asked him to deliver it. A surprise for Mr. Stone. I left it here because I didn't want it to get lost in the circus going on in the other room."

Even before he glanced into the bag, Jonah knew what he'd see, and there it was. Another little green box with a red ribbon. The third one of the day. Anger boiled up. He wanted to throw it against the wall, and he might have given in to the temptation, the momentary pleasure, if Cilla hadn't clamped a firm hand on his arm.

11

As Cilla pulled him into the corridor, Jonah still struggled to get a grip on his temper. It had been years since he'd totally lost it, not since that long-ago night when he'd been with Father Mike praying to the statue of St. Francis in the little prayer garden near the center and screaming curses at his father.

Cilla beamed a smile at Glenda and said, "We'll see you tomorrow night."

Her hand remained an iron clamp on his arm as she pulled him down the hall. A few doors down a family of three stepped out of their room and headed toward the elevators where several people, including Mark Gibbons, already stood waiting.

"Wonderful party," she said in the same tone that she'd used with Glenda. Bright, cheerful, as if neither of them had a care in the world.

Then she eased the gift bag out of his hand and slipped it over her arm. "It was so kind of them to give us a present."

Jonah looked at her then. She'd taken out her cell phone and was thumbing in a text message. Was it possible that she hadn't seen the green box inside the gift bag?

That thought shot straight out of his mind when she met his eyes. Hers were flat and coplike. She'd seen it all right.

She glanced down at her phone. He followed the direction of her gaze and read the text she'd written.

Play along with me. I feel like someone is watching us. I had the same feeling when we first arrived. I want you out of here before we open the boxes.

"But I'm so glad we're going home," she said in a voice that wasn't flat at all. It held promises.

Out of the corner of his eye, he saw two of the people waiting for the elevators glance their way.

Ignoring them, Cilla rose to her toes, clasped her hands on each side of his face and drew his mouth down to hers. She brushed her lips over his. "I have plans for when we get home."

While her breath feathered along his cheek and her scent twisted into him, Jonah decided there were ways to channel anger other than throwing things. "Let's give them something to watch." He jerked her closer and covered her mouth with his.

Cilla should have been prepared for the kiss. After all, she'd started it with the playacting. She'd sensed the fury in him and she'd wanted to deflect it.

Mission accomplished.

When he nipped her bottom lip and tightened his grip on her waist, heat streaked to her toes.

Confession time.

She hadn't just wanted to deflect his temper. She'd

wanted this. The fire streaking along her nerve endings, the glorious spiral of pleasure.

This was the kiss she'd wanted in the taxi, the one that she'd been hungering for the whole time she was watching him on that big screen at Interludes. There was no teasing, no gentle exploration, just raw demand. And all she wanted to do was meet it.

When his hands tightened again at her waist, she slid her own into his hair and moved in until her body was fully pressed against his. Then he lifted her off her feet.

All she could do was feel—the hard length of his thigh, the sharp angle of his hip, the quick beat of his heart. All she could hear was the hammering of her own heart—so loud that she wondered why people didn't run out of their rooms to quiet the racket.

Touch me. She wanted to shout it and hoped she hadn't. She should pull back. There was still a sane part of her mind that registered whispers and the giggle of a child. She was vaguely aware of the whoosh of elevator doors opening, people moving away, doors sliding shut again. But when he started to draw back, she gripped him even harder and took his mouth with hers.

Doors whooshed again, and she registered the sound of a gasp, then a deep chuckle.

"C'mon, Amanda, let's give the nice couple some privacy."

She drew back then and found that she was looking right into Jonah's eyes. What she saw—the heat, the recklessness—nearly had her damning the consequences and going back for more.

Someone coughed. "If you want, boss, I can get the two of you a room. We did a favor for one of the managers here a couple months ago."

Mark Gibbons. She'd forgotten he was there. He was

standing right behind Jonah, holding the doors of the elevator open. He'd seen everything. Embarrassment gave her the strength to release Jonah and get her feet fully on the ground. Not that she could feel them. But they did their job and propelled her into the elevator.

Jonah and Mark followed.

Punching the button for the lobby, she prayed that her voice would work. "We won't need a room. That was—" Several words flashed into her mind. A mistake? A show for anyone watching? The closest she'd ever come to having sex in a public place?

All of the above?

"Absolutely delightful," Jonah said, squeezing her hand.

She managed to shoot a glare at him before she said, "Can you stop the elevator before anyone else gets on?"

"Sure." He reached out and pushed a button. The car shuddered a little as it stopped.

Cilla turned to Gibbons. "With three of us watching, someone got this little gift bag into the Rubins' suite." She opened the bag so that Gibbons could see the green box. "I want to spread out our manpower. Someone gave it to the room service waiter and told him it was a surprise for Mr. Stone. I want you to find out what that waiter can remember and get a description."

"Maybe after our friend Tank delivered one box to the bell captain, he snuck back into the hotel through a service entrance and Santos missed him," Mark commented.

"That's what we want to verify, and a description would help."

Jonah leaned back against the door of the elevator and watched Cilla slip into Priscilla mode. Because the walls of the car had mirrors, he could see more than one of her as she fisted her hand on her hip and used the limited space to pace. He knew that she'd been just as affected by that kiss as he had. Her cheeks were still flushed, her voice just a little bit breathless. God, he had to admire the way she was able to snap right back into ace security agent.

"I want Santos to go back to the office and do some research on what was going on here in San Francisco at Christmastime six years ago," Cilla said. "Gabe has someone in his office digging into missing persons, mysterious deaths, etcetera in Denver, but maybe the motivation for the revenge is here and not in Denver. I'll contact Finelli and ask him to check into missing persons and unsolved and solved murders in December 2005."

Gibbons glanced down at the gift bag. "You going to wait for Santos to give you the other box and open them together?"

"I'm going to wait until we're clear of this place before we open either one. Once we get to the lobby, Jonah and I are going out the side entrance. I'll make sure we're not being followed before I hail a cab." She lifted the bag. "We'll take this and the other one to the office. Join us there when you're through."

"Why don't we meet at Pleasures instead?" Jonah asked. "We can all grab a bite to eat." He met Gibbons's eyes. "And I can assure you that the security at my club is excellent. Better than a nearly empty office building."

"Good point."

Jonah reached out and punched the button. A few seconds later, the doors opened and a family of five poured in. Once they alighted from the elevator in the lobby, Cilla waited only long enough for David Santos to hand her the other gift bag before pulling Jonah with her toward the side exit and out into the street. Darkness had settled over the city, but the pedestrian traffic was still heavy, and Cilla set a fast pace. She was angry. He could feel it radiating off her in waves, but she was not letting her emotions interfere with her job.

First she used her cell to call someone named T.D. Whoever it was made her laugh. The rich sound of it left that coppery taste in his mouth again. Next she called Finelli and told him what she needed. All the while, the path she cut through the heavy pedestrian traffic had them hugging the buildings, and at each intersection, she took a quick scan of the crowd behind them.

But she was ignoring the taxis.

"I know you're angry, partner. But don't you think it's time you filled me in on your plan? What are we doing?"

"Exactly what I said. I'm getting you away from the St. Francis without a tail."

"We're a good five blocks away from the hotel, and you haven't flagged a taxi yet."

"Sorry." She took a deep breath and let it out, and for the first time slowed their pace a bit. "You're right, I am angry. I got angry the instant Glenda handed you the gift bag and I saw another green box."

Remembering his own instant flash of blinding fury, he took her hand and squeezed it.

"If I hadn't been angry, I never would have…we never would have…"

"Kissed? But you complained that I didn't kiss you in the taxi."

"We shouldn't have kissed like *that*." At the corner, she swept her gaze to their rear, then strode into the street. "People were watching us. Mark was watching us."

"Well, I'm open to experimenting with other methods. Other techniques. Anytime."

She tried for a quelling look, but she had to swallow a sudden urge to laugh. "That's not what I'm talking about."

He smiled at her. "I'll have to persuade you, then."

She narrowed her eyes. "I thought you were interested in my plan."

"I'm interested in that, too."

This time the laugh escaped and some of her tension eased. "I made arrangements earlier for different transportation from the hotel."

"Different?"

"A friend of mine, T. D. Walters, is a partner in a private limo service."

He pulled her into the entranceway of a shop. "And just who is T.D.?"

She cocked her head to the side and studied him. "If it wasn't such a ridiculous idea, I'd say you were jealous."

"That is a ridiculous idea." But it didn't make it less true, Jonah decided.

"T.D. is a friend of mine." This time she spaced the words as if she were speaking to someone who didn't understand English. "When I worked for the SFPD, he was my first snitch. T.D. stands for Top Dog. I like him a lot, but he's not my type."

"I'm not your type, either."

She smiled at him. "Then the two of you should become best buds." After taking a quick scan of the street, she led the way onto the sidewalk again.

"I called T.D. when we were at Interludes because

I wanted to have a backup plan. Getting into a taxi in front of the St. Francis at this time of day makes it much too easy for someone to follow us." She waved a hand toward the bumper-to-bumper traffic on the street. "And this kind of congestion makes it all but impossible to lose a tail."

"But you didn't tell Gibbons or Santos about your limo plan."

"No. I wasn't sure I was going to use it. But I had a feeling we were being watched from the time we got to the hotel. Tank is still on the loose out there. And I'm more convinced than ever that he's working with someone."

She lifted the gift bags. "It doesn't take a Sherlock or a Watson to figure out where you're going to be today and that you'll eventually end up at Pleasures. Which has me wondering why the guy is choosing such public places to deliver the notes."

"A police station and the St. Francis when it would have been easier to drop them off at Interludes or even at Pleasures. My guess is he wants to show off how clever he is."

"And how vulnerable you are," she said. "He wants you to know he can find you anywhere."

"So when two boxes turn up at the St. Francis, the limo goes from being backup to Plan A," Jonah mused. "You want to show him he isn't as clever as he thinks he is."

"What I want to do is stop him."

He heard the anger flare in her voice again. Glancing at her, he watched her tamp it down and shrug it off. "And call me paranoid, but I don't want to give him a chance to watch while you open these. I think he likes to watch. That's another reason to choose public spaces to deliver the boxes."

Jonah thought of the detonator the police had found in the stairwell of the garage and of how many eyes would have been on them if he'd opened the boxes in the lobby or in the long taxi line in front of the hotel.

"We won't have to worry about watchers in the back-seat of T.D.'s limo," he said.

"Exactly."

A stinging mist had begun to fall. More than a few pedestrians had pulled out umbrellas. When they stopped for a red light at the corner, he said, "You didn't want me to open the box and read the note in the eleva-tor in front of Gibbons, either. Do you suspect that he or Santos might be involved in what's going on?"

"No." The look she shot him was one of surprise, but then she sighed. "I hate the fact that I even considered it. Or that I talked to Gabe about it. But he was already on it."

"I'm not surprised. I've considered them also. I can tell you that I don't think Gibbons is mixed up in this—even though he was working for G.W. Securities six years ago."

"Gabe says Santos was in the Marines six years ago and he worked with explosives. But there doesn't seem to be any connection to you."

"Has Gabe found any trace of my father?"

She sent him a sideways glance. "He thinks I ought to put you on that because you have superior skills at hacking."

"I can't imagine that someone who vanished from my life over twenty years ago would be interested enough to come back now. If he's even alive. When we get to the point that we're grasping at straws, I may give it a whirl."

"We could be approaching that point. Whoever is sending these little gifts is stepping up his game. It's still four nights before Christmas and he's given you three green boxes today."

He'd already given some thought to that himself. "He doesn't have to send just one note a day." He squeezed her hand. "We're going to figure this out."

"Okay. Okay. T.D. should be waiting for us up the block."

Top Dog Walters was just where he'd said he'd be, standing by the side of the limo when they turned into the alley. He was a large, powerfully built man with black hair that he wore pulled sleekly back into a ponytail. In the light thrown by the headlights, Cilla couldn't help but admire the neatly pressed chauffeur's uniform. It was a far cry from the ripped T-shirt and threadbare jeans she'd first seen him wearing during her days as a street cop.

There was more bling, too. He'd always favored a few earrings, but she was sure she spotted a new gold chain around his neck. The gold ring on his finger she'd seen before. In fact she'd watched his bride place it on his hand two years ago.

By the time she and Jonah reached him, he had the back door open. Then without further ado, he wrapped his arms around her and gave her a huge hug. "Sugar, it's been too long."

Releasing Cilla, he extended his hand to Jonah. "I'm T.D. Walters, by the way. And she saved my life."

Jonah shook the offered hand. "Jonah Stone. She may be in the process of saving mine."

"I didn't save T.D.'s life. I merely saw his potential

and introduced him to a friend who saw even more potential." Cilla poked a finger into T.D.'s chest. "And it didn't hurt your upward mobility that you married the boss's daughter. How's the new baby?"

"Beautiful, but she doesn't sleep much."

"I've heard that about a lot of babies." She gestured for Jonah to get into the limo first, then followed him. When T.D. had climbed behind the wheel, she said, "This is lovely, T.D. And it still has that new leather smell."

Turning in his seat, he beamed her a smile. "It's our top-of-the-line model. You can see out, but no one can see in. There's hot coffee in a thermos, wine, champagne, and there are some snacks in the cooler. Help yourself. I'll drive around. When you decide on a destination, let me know through the intercom." Then he pressed a button and the privacy screen lowered.

When the engine hummed to life and the limo started to move slowly forward, Cilla allowed herself one moment to lean back against the seat.

"Perfect plan, partner." Jonah reached over the two gift bags that lay on the seat between them and took her hand. "This is much better than the backseat of a taxi and we don't even have to break our ground rules."

"We don't?" Lord knew she wanted to, and what she saw in his eyes had her wondering why she'd ever established them in the first place.

"We agreed that making love again had to remain in the backseat until we solved the case." He gestured with his free hand. "This qualifies as a backseat, so I think we're good. But you'll probably want to open these boxes first."

It was more than heat she saw in his eyes. There was

humor and intelligence and an understanding that she'd never hoped to see. Never realized she wanted to see.

Releasing her hand, Jonah opened the box closest to him and read the note aloud, "'It's still four nights and counting. Have you remembered yet why you have to die?'"

Fear knotted in her stomach as she met his eyes again. "I'd say that was more than mildly threatening."

"As you said, he's stepping up his game." He lifted the second bag and was about to take out the green box when he suddenly frowned. "There's a tag on the bag. I didn't notice it earlier." Opening it, he held it for her to see. "It has your name on it."

Cilla thought back to the few minutes in the foyer when Glenda turned away to pick up the gift bag. She'd been totally focused on getting Jonah out of there. "Glenda said it was a surprise for Mr. Stone."

Jonah already had the box on his lap and was untying the ribbon. Inside was the same piece of folded, cream-colored paper that had been in the other four boxes. He flipped it open, then took her hand and held it as they read it together.

One night and counting... You've interfered with my mission for the last time. It's too bad that you won't live to see what I have in store for Jonah Stone.

12

"THIS CHANGES EVERYTHING," Jonah said.

"No." But for a second she couldn't unglue her eyes from the note.

One night and counting...

She forced herself to think and was pleased that her hand didn't tremble as she carefully took the note, re-folded it and placed it back in the green box. "It just means he's modified his plan."

"Modified?" Jonah took the box from her hands and put it on the leather banquette that ran along the side of the limo. Then he took her shoulders and turned her to face him. "That note is a death threat. That bastard is going to try to take you out."

She met his eyes. The fear she saw beneath the fury helped her settle and focus. "*Try* is the operative word. He's not going to succeed."

He gave her a little shake. "He sure as hell isn't. He isn't even going to get to try." He pulled out his phone. "I'm calling Gabe. He can send someone else out here. You're going to disappear until this is over."

She brought the edge of her hand down hard on his

wrist. The instant the cell phone dropped to the floor, she kicked it out of reach.

"Stuff that idea, partner. And if you go after the phone, I may have to really hurt you."

There was still anger in his eyes when he turned to face her, but she had his attention. And he was rubbing his wrist. "I want you out of this."

"And I've always wanted Santa Claus to be real. That's why I love the movie *Miracle on 34th Street*. You'll have to learn to live with the fact that I'm staying in." She poked a finger into his chest. "And you have only yourself to blame."

He frowned. "I know I'm to blame. I insisted you work on this, and now the guy wants to get rid of you so he can make a run at me."

She opened her mouth, then shut it. "I'm beginning to think that's not all of it."

"No, now he wants *you*."

"Not just that, either. He has this long-term plan to make you count down the six nights before Christmas. To make you wait and wonder and suffer before he makes his run. At the same time, he's giving the best security agency on this side of the country six days— now four—to track him down."

"What are you saying?"

She waved a hand. "He also wants this. He wants us to react, panic. Spin our wheels. If we decide to bring someone else in to bodyguard you, maybe bring in more protection for me, we're not totally focused on finding him."

"Dammit." Jonah sighed. "You could be right."

"Yeah. Look what happened after we discovered the bomb. No, he didn't succeed in blowing my car up, but the distraction still worked. I pulled Mark and David in to help protect you. They're the two best men I have and I kept them with us babysitting all day."

Jonah glanced at the green box. "If we'd opened that before we left the St. Francis, I wouldn't have let you send Gibbons and Santos off."

She followed the direction of his gaze. "Thank God for my attack of paranoia. But that note is still deflecting us. Everything he's done so far has split our attention. Hiring Mickey P. and Lorenzo to rough you up in the alley makes more sense now. He wanted you to bodyguard up."

"He didn't want them to get arrested."

"No. But then he delivers the second note to the police station and arranges for Tank to install the car bomb. All that directs our attention away from finding him. Whoever this guy is, he bounces back and he's not at a loss for ideas. He'll have other things up his sleeve."

Jonah took her hand, linked his fingers with hers. "We'll handle them, and we'll figure out who he is. Tonight, I'll try my hand at tracing my father."

She squeezed his fingers as something tightened around her heart. "It may be a wild-goose chase."

"Maybe it's time we went on a few." He met her eyes. "I'm not sending you away."

"Waste of time. I'm not going anywhere."

"I'm not forgetting that the number on your note was *one*. I don't intend to lose my partner."

"Remember that the next time you try to dump me, ace."

He laughed, then leaned in closer. "I also remember that we agreed to take a break after we opened the gift."

She placed a hand on his chest. "And I know exactly what you had in mind, but the clock is ticking here."

"Oh, I can be fast. Let me show you."

The thought of it sent a hot thrill right to her core. But his mouth was slow and soft as he brushed it over hers, and she couldn't prevent the sound that escaped.

"There's a practical side of you that thinks we should go back to Pleasures so that I can get started on tracing my father. I'm attracted to that part of you." He kissed the corner of her mouth. "I think of her as Priscilla. She wants to pull out her cell and check in with Gibbons and Santos." He kissed the other corner of her mouth.

Each time his mouth made contact, every pore in her body yearned.

"Then she'll want to touch base with Finelli." His teeth scraped along her jawline. "Then update Gabe. Have I left anything off Priscilla's list?"

She wasn't sure because every time his lips brushed hers, more of her thoughts faded.

"But I'm also attracted to the other side of you, the Cilla part. She isn't afraid to throw that to-do list away and risk everything for the moment. It was Cilla I found in the hotel bar in Denver. You're both of those women. I want you. Let me show you how much."

He whispered the words against her lips, the same words he'd said that night after he'd closed the hotel door.

"It's not that simple anymore." But her hand fisted his shirt.

"Then let's see where complicated takes us."

His mouth covered hers. Not softly this time. But she didn't want soft. There was nothing seductive about the way he was kissing her now. But she didn't want seduction.

She just wanted him.

"Touch me." She got the words out this time. Or he read her mind. For one wild moment, his hands seemed to be everywhere, inciting, arousing. In one fluid movement he had her out of her jacket and he pulled the sweater over her head. It might be cold outside, but she was suddenly plunged into hot, drenching summer. And she wanted to simply drown in it. He shifted her, then slid to his knees between hers to deal with her boots and slacks.

Shrugging out of his jacket, he brought his mouth back to hers, hot and greedy. She tasted hunger and desperation, but she wasn't sure whether it came from him or her.

And it wasn't enough. Not nearly enough.

She jerked his turtleneck free of his jeans and together they dragged it over his head. But before she could get her hands on him the way she'd imagined doing at Interludes, he gripped her hips and pulled her to the floor. Finally, his hands were on her bare skin, demanding, exploring, finding new pleasure points, rediscovering old ones. Wave after wave of pleasure washed through her until she knew only him—the taste, the feel, the smell of him.

Her heart had never beat this fast. Not even in that hotel room. And it still wasn't enough. She rolled, pushing him back into the soft carpet so that she could press kisses, quick and hungry, over his face, his neck, his chest. Everywhere.

Then he shifted, bringing his mouth to hers, and they rolled again.

More was all she could think.

More.

After a month of remembering, fantasizing, Jonah couldn't stifle his hunger. Nor could he seem to satisfy it. He simply had to touch and mold every inch of her with his hands, his mouth. Each separate sensation hammered through his blood and burned through his brain.

Her skin was softer than he'd remembered. It seemed to flow and then burn beneath his fingers. Her slender body enchanted him. Would he ever get enough of those long lean lines, the taut and ready strength, the delicate give of curves? They'd haunted his dreams for so many long silent nights.

Shifting, he pinned her against the side of the banquette and ran his hand up those slim thighs. She still wore her panties. He toyed with the edge. Lace. And he recalled the lace she'd worn on that long-ago night.

"Look at me, Cilla."

She did. They were eye to eye, and he could see himself in the cloudy green depths. He skimmed a finger beneath the lace. "I'm going to make you come, and then I'll make you come again. Tell me that's what you want."

She twined her arms around his neck. "Yes. That's what I want. I want you."

He slid a finger into her and then studied her face, watched the pleasure build in her eyes as his pulse beat in wild drumbeats. When he felt her crest, when he was sure she thought only of him, knew only the pleasure he was giving her, he shifted and rose to his knees to shove down his jeans and deal with the condom.

"Cilla."

She opened her eyes and that's all he could see—just the dark glint of them—as he lowered himself over her.

"Again," she whispered.

He entered her. As she closed around him hot and tight, the thought seared into his mind—she was everything. Everything he wanted. Then even that thought shattered as his control snapped.

The moment he began to move, Cilla gasped his name. The pleasure he'd already given her flashed to frenzy as he pounded into her with fast, powerful thrusts. Lost, unbearably thrilled, she matched him beat for beat. As new sensations tore through her, she raked her nails down his back and dug them into his hips, urging him on. This time, the orgasm built fast and ripped through her, filled her, and then seemed to empty her out.

She wasn't sure how long they lay there on the floor of the limo while her mind swam back to reality. But gradually she could absorb details—the hum of the motor, the muffled sounds of traffic. But she was also aware of the rapid beating of his heart against hers, his hair brushing her cheek.

And one of them had to break the silence. Bring reality fully into focus. "Did we just make love or war?"

She felt the curve of his mouth against her cheek. "I don't care what we call it. I want to do it again."

"Yeah." And as she felt him harden inside of her, she was outrageously tempted.

Then her cell phone rang. He rolled off her and took it out of her jacket. She frowned when she saw the caller ID and put it to her ear. "It's my apartment manager."

"Ms. Michaels?" The voice held annoyance.

Sitting up, Cilla held the phone so Jonah could hear. "Mrs. Ortiz, what is it?"

"Mr. Linderman called me to complain about the noise in your apartment. First, there was a loud crash, and now your music system is playing at full blast. I'm knocking on your door right now. Could you please turn it down?"

"I'm not in my apartment right now."

"Then who is making all that noise?"

"Good question," Jonah murmured as he gathered her clothes.

"I'm on my way." First, she hit the intercom button to give T.D. her address. "Fast as you can legally make it."

"I'll engage the rockets," T.D. said with a laugh.

"Our note sender may have broken into your apartment," Jonah said.

Mind racing, Cilla pulled on her sweater and slacks. "And then turned up my sound system to call attention to himself? More likely Flash did it."

"Flash?"

She grabbed her boots. "My cat. I call her that because when she wants to, she moves like lightning. She's not strictly speaking an alley cat, but close. When I moved in, she was living on the fire escape outside my apartment. I saw her through my living room window the day I moved in and made the mistake of feeding her. Next time I opened the window to the fire escape, she shot in. And stayed."

"And Flash knows how to operate your sound system?"

"She's learned exactly what button to push on the remote. She usually does it to get my attention when I'm working."

She joined him on the seat and did what she could to finger comb her hair. "I would have had to swing by the apartment anyway to pick up some clothes—for tomorrow and that fancy, schmancy thing of yours tomorrow night. And I'll fill Flash's dishes and lock up the remote. She'll be pissed, but at least Mr. Linderman and Mrs. Ortiz won't be."

Jonah laughed, slipping his arm around her and pulling her in for a quick hug. "Welcome back, Priscilla."

T.D. OPENED THE LIMOUSINE door, "Welcome to The Manderly Apartments." Cilla got out first and scanned the street.

"Clear," she said. Then she turned to T.D. "I know we weren't followed, but keep an eye out, will you? I've got you on speed dial, but call me on my cell if anyone comes into the building—even if it looks like they have a key."

"I got your back, sugar," T.D. said.

Jonah climbed out and took his own scan of the street. The night sky was clear enough to allow a quarter moon to wink through. Streetlights offered enough illumination for Jonah to realize that the neighborhood seemed familiar to him. The eclectic mix of architecture ranged from a church built along contemporary lines to an art deco building housing a bank and other shops.

But it wasn't until he swept his gaze over The Manderly Arms with its gothic architecture that the memory fully clicked. He'd taken morning runs right past the place. He even knew where the fire escape was—on the back corner of the building.

"Creepy place," he said as they walked toward the entrance. "Reminds me of that New York City apartment building in *Rosemary's Baby*."

"Wrong movie. Wait until you meet Mrs. Ortiz. She's a dead ringer for Mrs. Danvers in *Rebecca*."

He opened the front door, but he preceded her into the building, then stepped aside so that she could unlock the second door.

"How long have you lived here?" he asked.

"Since I moved back to San Francisco."

All those long nights when he'd stood at his window thinking of her, wanting her, she'd been only walking distance away. If he'd known, would he have climbed that fire escape?

Wasted time, he thought. And what if neither of them had much left to waste?

The lobby was a round, airy space with a circular staircase that rose to the second floor. A plump woman with steel-gray hair pulled back into a tight ballerina bun waited at the foot of it. She wore a black dress with a stiffly starched white apron over it. Her arms were folded, her expression disapproving.

"The music has stopped," she said. "But I want you to know that it was loud enough to hear all the way down here. It was playing 'We Need a Little Christmas.'"

"I'm so sorry. I don't know how it happened." Cilla waved a hand in the air as she moved past the woman and started up the stairs. "Probably a short in the electrical circuit. I'll unplug it until I can have it fixed."

As they rounded the first landing, Jonah saw Mrs. Ortiz was still frowning, and she was pointing one finger accusingly.

"I tried my master key," she called after them. "It doesn't work. You changed the lock. So I need a copy of your key," she said. "If I'd had one, I could have turned the music off myself."

"I'll get you one," Cilla called back. "Promise."

The loud *humph* followed them up the stairs.

Jonah spoke in a low voice. "You changed the lock on your apartment?"

"Pets aren't allowed."

His brows shot up. "You could move. There are pet-friendly places in San Francisco."

"I could move, but would Flash? Since she's never even let me pick her up, that could be a problem."

At the top of the stairs, she led the way down a hall-way so dimly lit that he could see slits of light spilling out from beneath closed doors. Only the murmur of TV shows marred the silence. At the last door, she stopped and pulled out her key. It was half an inch from the lock when she turned to him and held a finger to her lips.

She didn't have to tell him that she'd gotten one of her feelings, because he'd gotten it, too. Cold air pushed into the hall from beneath the door. Gesturing him to one side, she turned the key in the lock, then stepped to the other side and took out her gun.

She met his eyes, mouthed the word *Stay,* and then used her foot to open the door. He swept his gaze over the room as she fanned it with her gun. It was empty, but one of the panes on the window had been smashed, and a chubby-looking cat sat on the fire escape looking in.

Cilla, holding her gun in both hands, moved into the room. The feeling he'd had in the hall grew stronger, a hard clenching in his gut.

"Cilla?"

"Stay back until I check the kitchen and bedroom."

No way. He stepped through the doorway and caught a blur of movement before something slammed against his head and lights starred behind his eyes. He had a dizzying impression of the floor speeding toward him before there was nothing but black.

13

CILLA WHIRLED AT THE SOUND and saw that a large muscle-bound man had a gun pointed at Jonah's head.

His eyes were cold and very steady on hers. "Set your gun down easy, or I'll put a bullet in his brain."

"No problem." Very slowly, she lowered her weapon and squatted to set it on the floor as she took his measure. Early fifties, she thought. Gray hair cropped short. Both details matched the grainy images on the security tapes. His boots were scuffed, his jeans and the leather bomber jacket well-worn, but she bet the body beneath the clothes was well-toned. And there was a silencer on his gun.

At the edge of her vision, she saw blood blossom on the side of Jonah's head, but she pushed down on the flood of emotions that threatened and kept her voice very cool. "You're the man who drove the van last night at Pleasures and planted a bomb under my car."

"You're the woman who interfered with my mission."

There was temper in his tone. She might be able to use that. But he still had his gun pointed at Jonah's head. She had to get his attention and the weapon focused on her. So she laughed. "And your mission was?"

"That's for me to know."

"Where'd you hire those two goons you brought along? At 'Thugs R Us'?"

"Shut up," he said, swinging the barrel of the gun toward her. "I've already taken enough crap about that."

More temper, but this time it wasn't entirely aimed at her. She shifted to the balls of her feet, gauging the distance between them. She had to get closer if she was going to disarm him. "I imagine your boss was really pissed."

The man frowned. "He's not my boss. We're partners."

"A partner who sends you out on missions and lets you take all the risks?" She edged a step closer.

"Stop right there. I didn't come here to chat. You and I are going to take a little ride."

Even better, she thought as she took a step toward the door. If she could get him down to T.D.

"Not that way. You think I don't know you got a couple of agents out there waiting? I saw them following you earlier today. But I knew you'd have to come back here eventually."

Keep him talking, she decided. "And today's goal is to get me? Was that your decision or your partner's?"

"Mutual. Someone interferes with my mission, they pay."

"So you decided to enjoy some Christmas music while you waited?"

"Damn cat! I would have killed her but she was too fast."

He gestured with the gun. "We're going out the fire escape and right into my van. You first."

Turning, she walked toward the window and opened it. The faster she got him away from Jonah, the better.

Then she'd make her move. As she climbed out, she caught a glimpse of Flash on the level above them. Dropping her gaze, she gauged the distance to the cement floor of the alley. Too far to drop.

Then Tank was right there with her on the fire escape. "We're going down to the alley nice and slow. Try any of your tricks, like kicking the gun out of my hand, and I'll toss you off this thing."

She didn't doubt he'd try. Her mind racing, Cilla gripped the railing and started down the first flight of stairs. They creaked and swayed a little beneath her weight. The farther she could get him away from her apartment, the better. But she didn't like the idea of waiting to make a move until they reached the alley. Her chances of distracting him and taking him on the fire escape might be better.

On the second landing, she purposely missed a step and stumbled, lurching hard against the railing.

He snaked one arm around her neck, dragged her against him and squeezed hard. "You ever been shot in the gut?" He jabbed the gun into her waist. "I've seen men bleed out that way in Iraq. I can place a bullet where the pain will be excruciating."

Then he tightened the arm he had around her throat. Her vision grayed, but she managed to slip her hand into her pocket and press a number that would speed dial T.D. He'd take care of Jonah. But if she didn't find a way to delay the guy, he'd have her in the van and away from the building before T.D. could do a thing to help her.

When Tank finally released her so she could pull in a breath, she gripped the railing hard and let her knees sag.

"Let's go," he said.

"I need…a minute…here." She sagged harder against the railing and dragged in a ragged breath. Ego and temper. Those were his weak spots. She had to use them. Fast.

JONAH LIFTED HIS HEAD and opened his eyes. Pain spiked at his temple and the room spun once before he could focus on the details. The one that struck him first was the plump cat perched on the back of the couch.

Flash. That's what Cilla had called her. She hadn't been in the room when they'd arrived, and the window behind her hadn't been open. Just the pane had been broken.

Panic joined the pain as he got to his feet. "Cilla?"
No response.

How long had he been out? Long enough for whoever had hit him to get Cilla.

Flash shot out through the window and landed gracefully on the railing. When he reached the sill, he leaned out and followed the direction of the cat's gaze.

For a moment, his heart stopped. Two landings below, Cilla leaned against the railing and a man the size of a small Mack truck stood a few feet away. He had a gun aimed at her.

He wanted to call out, get the man's attention on him, but he knew Cilla well enough now to be certain that she'd use the distraction to attack. And while he'd seen some of her moves and knew she had skill and strength, the man was huge, the space was small and they were still two stories off the ground.

A sound had him whirling to see T.D. standing in the open doorway of the apartment.

Jonah put a finger to his lips, then motioned him to the window and pointed. He didn't have to say much to fill in T.D. The man with the gun aimed at Cilla spoke volumes.

"Distraction," T.D. whispered.

"First, I want to get out there and move closer," Jonah whispered back. "Once I'm close enough, crank on the sound system again."

T.D. nodded, and Jonah very carefully ducked low and moved one leg out onto the fire escape.

"I CAN SEE YOU'RE A LOT smarter than your two employees," Cilla said, spacing her words and keeping her voice raspy. "But your partner is the one with the real brainpower."

"What are you saying?"

"You're here. And he's not."

"So? This is what I'm good at."

"And he's good at staying out of sight. He's the one who takes care of sending the little green boxes, right?"

"Yeah. He's good at strategy and planning. I'm good at the actual combat."

"And it's always the combat people who put their lives on the line. Your partner doesn't even deliver the boxes in person. He's a ghost, but you've been spotted. The camera at the garage where you planted the bomb this morning got a good shot of your face, an even better one of your license plate. I'm surprised the police haven't picked you up yet."

His grin was quick and crooked, the swagger in his tone clear. "Because I'm too smart for them. I changed the license plates."

"How about your name? I sure hope you've got a second ID up your sleeve."

Something in his eyes told her she'd hit the nail on the head.

"But no one knows who your so-called partner is." She sent him a pitying smile. "He's smoke."

"I know who he is."

She could see she had him thinking now. Just then she caught a blur of movement above and saw Jonah climb out onto the fire escape.

And Tank still had the gun.

Ready or not, she had to make her move now. No space to use her foot.

He started at the sudden blare of music. She fisted the hand she'd kept on the railing and rammed it hard against his gun hand.

The exploding bullet made her ears ring, but the gun sailed away, and he took a quick step back. Ducking her head, she sprang forward and bulldozed into him with enough force to send him back against the wall of the building. The impact had pain singing from her shoulder and down her arm.

He didn't even grunt. Instead, he yelled, "Bitch!"

Even as she jumped back onto the balls of her feet, footsteps thundered on the stairs above them. Before she could aim a kick at his groin, he rushed her, grabbing her shoulders and lifting her off her feet.

Then she was suddenly dangling feetfirst over the railing, and the only thing preventing her from falling like a rock were the ham-size hands gripping her shoulders.

For a split second, they were face-to-face, eye-to-eye. His gleamed with fury. She didn't struggle, letting her arms hang loose.

"Told you I'd toss you over." He bit out the words, then pulled his hands away.

She grabbed for the railing and caught it with one hand. The wrong hand, she decided as the pain started singing again in her shoulder. But she held on and wrapped the fingers of her other hand around an iron post.

When she glanced up, she saw he had his fist raised, ready to hammer it down hard on her hand. Mentally, she prepared for the fall. Hit, tuck and roll.

Then there was a blur of movement. Flash landed on his shoulder and went for his face.

The man's scream pierced the night as his hands flew upward and he whirled. Off balance, he lurched against the railing, then pitched over and dropped.

When Jonah heard the sound of the body hitting the cement, his heart leaped to his throat and stayed. Not Cilla, he told himself. She was still clinging to the railing. He rounded the last landing and took the steps three at a time, jumping over the cat on the last one. Then he gripped her wrist with both hands. "Got you."

"Let me help." T.D. leaned over the railing and grabbed her other wrist.

Jonah's heart was still pounding in his throat as together they hauled Cilla up until she could get her leg securely over the railing. Then he pulled her into his arms and simply held on. Until his legs began to tremble. Lowering himself to one of the stairs, he shifted her onto his lap.

"I'll check on the scumbag." T.D. started down the next flight of steps.

Overhead, "Angels We Have Heard on High" blasted into the cold night air while feelings poured through him—he couldn't even begin to name them all. He hadn't allowed himself to feel them for years. Not since that night he'd stood in the small prayer garden with Father Mike and railed at the statue to bring his father back so that he could kill him.

Everything, he thought. He'd nearly lost everything that mattered to him. Again.

When Cilla stirred in his arms, he managed to take one steady breath.

She tipped back her head and met his eyes. "Are you all right? I saw the blood on your head, but I couldn't afford to keep him in the apartment. His temper was too volatile."

"You think?" He framed her face with his hands and allowed himself to take one desperate kiss. *Mine,* he thought. And this time the word hummed in his blood until it settled in his heart.

He drew back just far enough to lay his forehead on hers. "You scared me, Cilla."

"Back at you."

Maybe, in a hundred years or so, he'd get the image of her hanging over the edge of the railing out of his mind. A few hundred more and he might rid himself of that feeling that he wasn't going to be on time. Right now, all he could do was hold on.

"There are definitely two of them in on this," Cilla said. "Tank isn't an employee. He claims to be a partner. We need to get a name from him."

"This guy needs an ambulance," T.D. called up.

Rising, Jonah set Cilla on her feet, keeping one arm around her as they moved to the railing.

Tank was lying faceup on the cement and T.D. was pulling out his cell phone. "He's breathing, but he hit his head in the fall and he's bleeding like a pig."

Overhead the music segued into "We Need a Little Christmas." Flash leaped up to the railing next to Jonah.

Jonah ran a hand over the cat. "You do good work, Flash."

Above them, the music went suddenly silent. Mrs.

Ortiz poked her head out the window of Cilla's apartment. Flash jumped down and settled in between Jonah's and Cilla's legs.

"I've warned you about that music, Ms. Michaels. I'm going to have to call the landlord."

Cilla hissed, "She's in my apartment—she'll see the cat food, the toys. I'm so busted."

"A tank with a gun doesn't bother you, but your landlady does." Then he turned to call up the stairs. "There was an intruder in the apartment. Ms. Michaels is calling the police."

"Right. Finelli." Cilla pulled out her cell.

"The police?" Mrs. Ortiz sounded shocked.

Stooping down, Jonah lifted up Flash and settled her into the crook of his arm.

"The intruder had a gun and he would have gotten away if it hadn't been for the intervention of this cat," he called up. "Must live in the alley back here."

Cilla shifted her gaze from him to the cat and muttered, "She never lets me pick her up."

"An intruder, you say?" Now the landlady sounded horrified. "This is a safe neighborhood."

"I'm sure you'll want to inform the landlord," Jonah said.

"Yes. Of course. I'll do that right away. And the police are coming?"

"They're on their way," Cilla assured her.

When Mrs. Ortiz's head disappeared, Jonah murmured, "Distraction works wonders."

Down in the alley, T.D. muffled a laugh. "The two of you go on up," he said. "I'll babysit the trash until the police get here."

14

IT WAS NEARLY NINE O'CLOCK before Cilla and Jonah entered his apartment above Pleasures. They might have been delayed even longer, but once Finelli had taken their statements, he'd allowed her some time to pack what she needed. Then he'd personally escorted them to T.D.'s limo and ordered them to go into lockdown at Jonah's place. He'd call them there with any updates or new questions.

The EMTs who'd arrived with the ambulance hadn't been able to report much on the injured man's condition except that he was unconscious and might have fractured his skull. Finelli had tracked down a name from the set of Colorado license plates that he'd found inside the van. It matched the registration of the van, which belonged to a Paul Michael Anderson. Finelli had also sent two uniforms to the hospital with Anderson.

So they had a name now, but not much else. And ever since they'd arrived at his apartment, she and Jonah had been on their cells or on a wide-screen conference call with Gabe.

She had to award Jonah's apartment kudos for pacing room. No walls marred the long expanse of honey-colored parquet floors. Lovely arched windows ran the length of one wall and offered a cushioned window seat and a distant view of the bay. You had to love a place where you could sit and just stare out at the water and think. Flash had settled in one of the window seats for a while after they'd arrived. But when Jonah had moved to his desk to work, she'd decided to curl up at his feet.

Cilla swept her gaze over the space again. When she'd been here the first time, her mind had been on business. But even then she'd noticed the economical way the apartment was designed. At the far end a marble counter blocked off a galley-size kitchen. The balconied loft space above held two bedrooms and two baths.

In the center of the apartment, a comfortable-looking U-shaped couch sat in front of a brick fireplace and a large flat-screened TV. Closer to the entrance was the office space Jonah was using now with its state-of-the-art equipment. Across from it was a steel-and-glass conference table that could also be used for dining.

She sank down on a chair at the conference table. The room-service waiter had claimed it was a woman who'd given him the gift bag to deliver, but he'd been short on details. Mark Gibbons was checking out Paul Michael Anderson, and David Santos's summation of December 2005 in San Francisco was that babies had been born, old people had died, but there didn't seem to be anything that could be related to the St. Francis Center for Boys, or Jonah. So far, Gabe hadn't found any more than that in Denver. His fiancée, Nicola Guthrie, was checking into FBI records.

In short, they were still spinning their wheels, and the clock was ticking.

During their conference call with Gabe, it had been

Jonah who'd asked what his friend had been able to find out about his father, and Gabe had offered to send what he had, but he'd warned them that it was a series of dead ends.

Basically, Darrell Stone had ceased to exist shortly after he'd last visited Jonah and his mother in Denver. Gabe had been able to trace him to Texas and then to Phoenix. But after that, there was no credit card trail, no evidence of anyone using that social security number ever again. And there was no death certificate, either. Nothing.

Jonah had decided to try to trace his father prior to the last time he'd visited his family, and he'd been at it for quite a while. Flash still lay curled at his feet.

As she leaned toward him, he glanced up. "I don't think I'm going to find my father."

"Do you think he must be dead?"

"There's no death certificate under that name. I've located a birth certificate for Darrell Jonah Stone, and I have death certificates for his parents, who died when he was eighteen. But I haven't been able to find much else. Gabe was able to dig up information on his credit card transactions after he left that last time twenty years ago, so I dug a little deeper, but I can't find records of his using that card anywhere but in the Denver area."

"So what did he use during the times when he was away from you and your mom?" Cilla asked.

"Good question. But I found something even more interesting. His Colorado driver's license and his car registrations only date back thirty years. I can't find any previous registration or license under that name from any other state. Even more interesting is the fact that his social security number was also issued thirty years ago. According to the birth certificate, Darrell Stone would be fifty-eight now."

As she turned the information over in her mind, she got up and began to pace in the small space between Jonah's desk and the conference table. "Thirty years ago. That's about the time when he would have met your mother at that party and it was love at first sight."

"That's right."

She turned and met his eyes. "What do you make of it?"

He leaned back in his chair and folded his hands behind his head. "One theory I'm entertaining is he created enough of an identity for himself to be able to get a marriage license and live in Denver as Darrell Stone, but during the times he was away, he lived as someone else."

"Why would he do that?"

"That's the big question. He said he worked for the government."

Cilla studied him for a moment. She knew that Jonah had recently worked with Gabe and their friend Nash Fortune to find and reunite a family living in the Witness Protection Program. She had been providing security for part of that family when she'd met Jonah at the Fortune Mansion in Denver that first day. "You're not thinking witness protection."

He shook his head. "No. If you're in the Witness Protection Program, you have to stay put or they kick you out. It's possible he was a bigamist. Maybe he had a family here and another one somewhere else. There are men like that."

"But they usually don't stop juggling the families and living multiple lives until someone discovers the bigamy. And they usually get outed and prosecuted. So why didn't you hear about it? Or why didn't he come back and try to explain?"

"There's always the chance that he was telling the truth. He did work top-security jobs for the government and for some reason he wanted to keep his marriage and his family a secret. But even that theory doesn't answer why he didn't come back."

Something tightened around her heart, and she walked to him and took his hand in hers. "I'm sorry that I opened up this whole can of worms for you."

"I'm not sorry. I thought I'd stopped being angry at my father years ago, but I think I just buried it. And not trying to find him was a good way to keep that anger buried. But now I'm curious."

"If he was using two identities, it could be that there's a death certificate, just not under Darrell Stone."

"I know." He smiled.

She saw the light in his eyes and felt a little tingle along her nerve endings. "But you don't think he's dead, do you?"

"No."

She pulled a chair from the conference table and sat down across from his desk. "Talk to me."

"It's just a feeling that's been growing since you prodded me into looking for him. Lord knows, I've wanted him to be dead." He put his hands on his face, rubbed his eyes. "You know, I once prayed that I would find my father, but it was so I could kill him."

"How old were you?"

"I was thirteen and I'd bounced through a couple of foster homes, run away a couple of times. A judge who'd gotten tired of seeing me in her court sentenced me to a year of going to the St. Francis Center every day after school and on Saturdays. She threatened—no, promised me that if I didn't give my foster home and the center at least a year, she'd send me away to a juvenile detention facility. I saw in her eyes that she meant it.

"But I was still so angry. There was this statue of St. Francis in a little prayer garden. It was close to Christmas during the first year I was going to the center. I liked Father Mike and I was getting to know Nash and Gabe. But Father Mike could sense my anger. On Christmas Eve, he took me to the statue of St. Francis. He told me that I should say the prayer in my heart, to ask for something that I really wanted. So I did. I shouted the prayer out loud. I prayed to St. Francis to bring my father back to me so that I could kill him. All I could think of was that Christmas when we'd waited and waited for him. And I wanted him to be dead for leaving my mother and me."

Cilla covered his hand with hers, and when he turned his to link their fingers, she held on. "Understandable. There were times when I entertained fantasies of making my father suffer because he was always too busy at Christmas and he made my mother so unhappy."

"The problem is that the statue of St. Francis I prayed to has special prayer-granting powers. My friends Gabe and Nash—their prayers have all been answered. The church where the statue now resides has become a Mecca for tourists."

"So...you not only think he's alive, you think you're going to find him."

"Something like that. I hope to God I'm not going to end up killing him."

"For what it's worth, I don't think he's mixed up in what's going on now."

When the phone on his desk rang, Jonah reached for it. "Yes, Virgil? Sure, bring Carmen and Ben up." He turned to Cilla. "Virgil says that Carmen might have the answer to a question you were asking her earlier today."

Cilla got that clutch in her gut the instant that Carmen stepped off the elevator. Ben, a tall young man with dark hair and his mother's smile, followed her. He had a laptop tucked beneath his arm. Bringing up the rear of the small parade was Virgil pushing a cart.

"I brought refreshments," he announced, and then began to unload trays of sandwiches and drinks on the glass table.

Carmen spoke to Jonah first. "I've got Dickie and Pete covering the closing of the club. But when Ben called and told me he remembered something from six years ago at the St. Francis Center, I thought you'd want to know right away."

Jonah moved from behind his desk to take her hands. "You did the right thing. Cilla and I feel like we've been bumping into brick walls all day." He turned to Ben. "Why don't you show us what you've got?"

"Photos mostly. I was pretty snap-happy in those days. Father Mike asked me to record most of the events at the St. Francis Center. He got me the camera and provided the film. When I looked through the pictures I started to remember."

A flush spread over Ben's face as he spoke. "There was this young woman who volunteered at the center. She was eighteen or nineteen. I was fourteen and a little immature."

"Smitten is what you were—puppy love," Carmen said as she placed a hand on her son's arm. "The first time it hits you, you fall hard. And Ben had it bad.

When he brought his laptop into Interludes and showed me some of the pictures, I started to remember, too."

"And you thought Ben's crush might connect to what's happening now," Cilla prodded.

Ben glanced at his mother. "The thing is, as big a crush as I had on this girl, she had an even bigger one on Jonah. She was a volunteer. She helped out in the office and sometimes she worked with the younger boys. But whenever Jonah was there, she practically stalked him. I didn't stand a chance. She was following him while I was sort of doing the same thing with her—but with my camera."

He held out a photo to Jonah. "I brought my laptop, but when I came across this one, I blew it up and printed it out. Mom told me about the presents you've been receiving, and I thought you'd want to see this."

Cilla moved to Jonah's side as she studied the picture. In it a young blonde woman stood in front of a Christmas tree. The camera had caught her in profile, offering a gift to Jonah—a green box tied with red ribbon.

Cilla felt it then. Not a tingle, but something pushing at the edge of her memory.

"Do you remember her?" Ben asked.

"Vaguely," Jonah said. "Let's see if we can connect the laptop to the TV and we can view the pictures on the big screen." He led Ben over to the U-shaped couches in front of the TV.

Carmen turned to Cilla. "I may be making a mountain out of a molehill, but you said to tell you anything that seemed out of the ordinary about that Christmas season six years ago."

"I did."

"You think what's going on now goes back that far?" Virgil asked.

"It's a theory," Cilla said.

"I was here in the San Francisco area back then," he said. "Jonah opened Pleasures the summer of 2006, and he hired me away from a sweet little place in Sausalito where I'd been tending bar for a couple of years."

"I was here, too. Fresh out of the police academy, my first year on the streets." Cilla felt something again— just a little tug. "Jonah was here in San Francisco, too. He was looking for this building. Can you stay for a while, Virgil, and look at Ben's pictures?"

"Sure." Virgil crossed to Jonah's desk phone. "I'll just let my assistant manager know where to call me."

A few minutes later, they were all seated on the couches in front of the flat-screen TV over the fireplace. Ben tapped keys on his laptop and a series of photos began to appear.

"Mom told me to start with December," Ben explained.

There were candid shots of a Christmas party in progress—kids of various ages opening presents, eating cake. Jonah was in a couple of them handing out presents. And she was pretty sure she spotted her boss, Gabe Wilder, dressed up as Santa and wearing a beard.

There were posed shots, one with a large group standing around the Christmas tree, another with the priest she knew as Father Mike standing with a smaller group around a statue of St. Francis. They were all wearing coats and hats and waving at the camera.

"The Christmas party was early that year, and the weather was mild," Ben said. The next series of shots were all taken on the basketball court. Once again, Cilla was able to recognize Jonah and Gabe. They seemed to be refereeing games for the boys and girls who went to the center.

But there was another person who was beginning to look familiar, too, a tall, slender young woman. The same woman Ben had captured handing the present to Jonah. She wasn't young enough to be one of the kids. And not pretty exactly. You might not have been able to pick her out in a crowd except for the long blond, Alice-in-Wonderland hair.

Cilla felt the tug again.

"I do remember that girl," Jonah said. "Her name was Elizabeth something."

"Baxter. Elizabeth Baxter," Ben said. "I didn't have the courage to even say a word to her. Not that she would have paid any attention to me. She only had eyes for you, Jonah."

Jonah frowned. "Nice girl. Quiet. I was so busy then, working part-time at G.W. Securities, still volunteering at the center, and trying to line up places that Mrs. Fortune and I could see in San Francisco." He paused, his frown deepening. "I'd forgotten all about her. But earlier that fall, someone had started leaving notes in my mail slot at the center. All of them signed by a secret admirer."

"What kind of notes?" Cilla asked.

"Silly stuff. Poems, sometimes with pictures of flowers on them. I just ignored them. I figured they were harmless enough."

Ben clicked on his keyboard and brought up a shot of the young blonde woman putting an envelope in a mail slot. "Here I am, super stalker in action."

Jonah rose to his feet, moved closer to the TV screen. "Then there were gifts—little things—a paperweight with my initials, a framed photo of Gabe and me shooting some hoop. I still didn't think anything of it. I was too busy."

When Ben brought up the picture of Elizabeth handing Jonah the green box, Cilla moved to his side. "What was in the box?"

"A ring. And a note telling me that she'd fallen in love with me. That we were destined to be together."

"What did you do?" Cilla asked.

"Father Mike had had to leave the party early to say a vigil mass at the Capuchin monastery. But I felt that I had to do something immediately, so I asked Gabe to stay. He and I met with her together after the party, and I gave her back the ring. I talked to her. Or tried to. I told her that what she was going through was normal. We all get a crush on somebody. It's part of growing up."

"That's the same speech that Mom gave me," Ben said.

"Not that it worked," Carmen said. "Puppy love is tough."

"Well, with Elizabeth, what I said seemed to work. She said something about some people being destined to be together, and that when we died and came back in another lifetime, we would find each other. I don't know what I'd expected, but when she left, she was smiling. And Gabe thought I'd handled it pretty well."

Pausing, Jonah ran a hand through his hair. "I never thought any more about it. That night I left for San Francisco to scout out places for Mrs. Fortune to look at. Finding the right building and making Pleasures a reality kept me away from the center for a while. When I finally did go back, she wasn't there anymore."

"She stopped coming to the St. Francis Center before Christmas," Ben said. "She told everyone that she was moving away. The day she made the announcement, I took several shots. To remember her by." He brought up more photos on the screen.

Cilla's stomach knotted as she moved closer to the TV. She tapped a finger on one of the images. "Can you enlarge this one, Ben?"

"Sure."

As soon as he did, the memory that had been nagging at her slipped into place and her stomach sank.

"She cut her hair," Cilla said.

"Yeah," Ben said. "Everyone was kind of shocked. But she said she was about to begin a new life and she was leaving everything about her old life behind. She was so looking forward to starting fresh."

"I'm pretty sure I remember her, too," Cilla said. "I didn't recognize her when she had the long hair because it was short like this when I first saw her. If I'm right, she did leave her old life behind. And she did it right here in San Francisco."

She paused to study the picture on the screen again. But it was almost a perfect match to the one she'd carried in her head for years. Moving closer, Jonah linked his fingers with hers.

"She was one of the first cases I was assigned to during my rookie year on the force," Cilla went on. The details flooded into her mind. "Joe Finelli was my partner then. It was Christmas Eve and we'd pulled the night shift. We got the call around late Christmas Eve. A drowning. We weren't sure where she went in, but her body was discovered floating beneath one of the piers. A Jane Doe. No ID. No one in the area was ever reported missing."

"I remember reading about it," Virgil said. "A couple

of days after Christmas, an artist's sketch ran in the local papers. On TV, too."

"We never got an ID," Cilla said. "All she had on her was a note. It had been sealed in waterproof laminate. It read, 'I'm leaving for a whole new life. This time I'll be with my true love.'"

"Good Lord," Jonah murmured. "She committed suicide because she believed it was the only way she could be with me? How could that possibly be?"

"If she was into that reincarnation stuff, she might have believed that dying was the fastest way to get to the next life where you and she could be together," Ben said.

Carmen put an arm around her son. "Or it could be that she was a total nutcase. All the loonies are not in the loony bin."

Cilla kept her fingers linked with Jonah's when she turned to Ben. "Did Elizabeth ever mention any relatives?"

"Not to me directly," Ben said. "I never did get up the nerve to talk to her. But when she worked with the younger kids, she used to tell stories about her twin brother and her uncle. They were both in the military."

"If she was telling the truth, we should be able to trace them." Jonah moved to his computer.

"I'll update everyone else," Cilla said, pulling out her cell.

Virgil gestured to Carmen and Ben. "You guys are coming with me. The chef has a dessert he's creating tonight for the staff to test."

At 3:00 a.m., he sat in his car and watched as the lights at Pleasures blinked off one by one. Except for those on the third floor.

They were still on. The two of them were still working, trying to find out who he was.

His fingers tightened on the steering wheel as he pushed down hard on the anger. Thanks to the bungling of his partner, they had to be one step closer to identifying him. When the red mist appeared in front of his eyes, he blinked it away.

He'd nearly given in to his anger when he'd seen what had happened in the alley outside Cilla Michaels's apartment. From his vantage point at the mouth of the short alley, the plan he'd devised had seemed to be going according to schedule.

Cilla was leading the way down the fire escape. And the limo driver who'd dropped them off was pacing at the front of the building, checking his messages on his phone.

Then his partner had changed the plan. Suddenly, Cilla was dangling feetfirst over the railing. He was supposed to kidnap her and kill her someplace else. So they would have to look for her and spin their wheels.

And Jonah Stone would know what it was like to lose someone he loved.

But the plan might still have worked. The drop from the second story could have killed her. It would certainly have injured her and caused Stone both suffering and distraction.

But she hadn't been the one who'd dropped to the cement in the alley.

She hadn't been the one who'd been taken away unmoving in an ambulance.

The red mist had blurred his vision several times as he'd followed the ambulance to its destination. An emergency room. So his partner was alive. But the police would have his fingerprints. They'd be able to trace his identity.

That would take time. And it would take even more time for them to put things together and find him. If they ever did.

As one of the lights blinked off on the third floor of the club, his hands tightened on the steering wheel again. They were going to go to bed now. And they'd make love. This man who should have loved Elizabeth would make love with the woman who was trying to spoil everything.

And they shouldn't be sleeping. This was time they were supposed to spend chasing their tails. And it wasn't his partner's fault. No, it was the woman's fault. He'd had the perfect plan. But she wasn't supposed to be in it.

Time, he reminded himself as he rested his forehead against the steering wheel. It was still on his side. And he was good at measuring people and finding their vulnerabilities. A new plan began to form in his mind. He could still take her out of the picture. Still make Stone experience what it was like to lose the person you loved most in the world.

He could still avenge Elizabeth's death.

Tomorrow night at Pleasures.

15

THE APARTMENT WAS SILENT except for the hum of his computer. Jonah studied the two screens on his desk. They were scrolling and sifting through data. As soon as Carmen and her son had left, Finelli had called to report the bad news that the name Paul Michael Anderson was an alias with a driver's license, a car registration and a social security number that only dated back one year. Cilla had contacted Gabe to report on their progress and divide up the work. Gabe was digging into Elizabeth Baxter, and he wouldn't be reporting in until he was sure he had everything.

Jonah had opted for the more complicated assignment, tracking down who Paul Michael Anderson really was. Following his best hunch, he was running the photo on Anderson's driver's license through military databases, hoping for the real name to pop.

Which would take time.

A glance at the bottom of his computer screen said 3:00 a.m. Time to call it a night. Flash had deserted him for one of the window seats over an hour ago. He turned in his chair, intending to tell Cilla it was time for a break, and he saw that she'd already fallen asleep on the couch. Rising, he moved closer.

Moonlight fell in rectangular patches across the floor. Other than that the room was dark, save for the dim glow from a table lamp and the computer screens. She lay curled up like a child, her hand beneath her cheek. Her face looked fragile, her wrists delicate. He'd never thought of her as either, he realized.

It had been her aura of strength and of competence that had drawn him from that first meeting of eyes. But he'd never watched her sleep before. Not even in the dreams that had haunted him for so many long silent nights. But when he'd dreamed of her, when he'd tossed and turned hoping to find her in his bed, sleeping had never been part of his fantasy.

No, what he'd wanted more than anything was a repeat of that long, sexy night they'd spent in that hotel room in Denver. Wanted it with a desire that had begun to boil in his blood. Looking at her now, he couldn't bring to mind why he'd waited so long to go to her and take what he'd wanted. What he still wanted.

Only now, he wanted more. And he knew that the wanting wasn't going to stop. The qualities he was seeing in her as she slept, the vulnerability that she kept so carefully hidden were pulling at him and arousing him even more than the fearlessness that he found so admirable.

When he reached the couch, he dropped to his knees and pushed a dark curl of her hair off her forehead.

She stirred, just as he wanted her to. And when she opened her eyes, he watched the cloudiness of sleep fade into recognition and desire.

I want you. Neither of them had to say the words aloud. Keeping his eyes on hers, he took her hands and drew her up with him as he rose to his feet. They undressed each other in silence, not touching except for the brush of a fingertip—on his chest, at her waist. Over his shoulder, down her arm.

Cilla had been dreaming of him before he'd awakened her, wanting him with the same intensity that she'd been experiencing for so many nights. When he'd touched her to push her hair back, she'd thought for a moment that she was lost once again in the dream that she'd had for so long. Her mind had already been filled with him, her body heated in anticipation. But this time she wasn't dreaming of his touch. He was real.

Moonlight slanted through the narrow windows. She loved how the mix of light and shadow heightened the desire and the pleasure she saw in his eyes. And when he skimmed his gaze over her, her heart began to thud.

In silence still, he stepped out of his slacks and she out of hers. Then she moved into his arms and pressed herself against him. "Jonah." His name was a quiet sigh as she cupped his face with her hands and brought his mouth to hers.

But he didn't kiss her, not in the way he'd done in her dreams. Not in the way he'd ever done before. He kept the pressure soft, taking her hands from his face and linking his fingers with hers as they sank to their knees.

His mouth was so warm, his lips so gentle, coaxing and teasing, only taking more when she sighed his name again. No one had ever kissed her like this—as if he had all the time in the world and intended to take it. Only Jonah, she thought as ribbons of pleasure unwound through her system. And when he released her hands and began to touch her, there was such tenderness in his fingers that it might have been starlight only moving over her skin.

Even as she began to float, emotions welled up in her. Her eyes stung, her throat burned, and the liquid yearning he was building in her sprang as much from her heart as from her body.

Home, she thought, and the silent sound of the word in her head trembled through her. She didn't want him to be a dream anymore. The dream would never be enough. Ever.

Jonah used his hands gently to touch, explore, exploit. He knew her now. During all those sexy silent nights when he'd relived every moment in his imagination, he'd had the time to review and file away what pleased her most. What made her catch her breath, what made her sigh. And each time she did, he offered more. Took more.

His heart ached to tell her what he was feeling. But he wasn't sure she was ready to hear the words. Or whether he was ready to say them aloud.

But at least he could show her.

Lowering her to the floor, he used his mouth on her. Each time she trembled, his heart pounded harder and his blood burned hotter. Still, he forced himself to keep the pace slow. Torturing himself as well as her, he took the time to savor the flavors of her skin, the saltiness of her neck, the honeyed sweetness of her breast. He lingered there for as long as he could. But his hunger was building for more. Her taste grew darker at her waist, darker and richer still as he moved lower. And when he nudged her thighs apart and found her core, he feasted.

She erupted. When her body quaked and reared, he tightened his hold on her hips, and when she settled, he began to build the pleasure again—slowly, steadily.

When she was close to a climax again, when he could feel every muscle in her body tightening, reaching, he moved up and over her.

"Cilla?" he whispered.

When she opened her eyes, he looked into them and saw everything he was looking for. And he filled her.

She groped for his hands, linked her fingers with his. "Everything."

The sound of the breathless word filled the air, and still Jonah fought for control. Her eyes stayed open and on his as each thrust brought them both closer.

And when he was flying off the edge, reeling, his mouth moved to hers and whispered her name as they fell together.

CILLA FOUND HERSELF SINGING in the shower. Twice. The first time was before Jonah had joined her. After the night they'd spent together, she hadn't thought it possible to want him again so desperately. But she had.

And now she was singing again.

So what?

She might be falling in love with a man who had three strikes against him. She pressed a panicked hand against her heart. She was not going to think about that now. She didn't have time.

Gabe had called from the airport. He'd flown in with Father Mike Flynn and they were on their way to Pleasures. Finelli had called next. He was bringing over the cold-case file on Elizabeth Baxter. Cilla didn't have time to sing anymore.

When Jonah opened the bathroom door, she pulled the shower curtain in front of her and pointed a finger. "Stay right where you are." The fact that he was fully dressed didn't fool her. He'd been fully dressed in different jeans and T-shirt when he'd joined her the first time. "Gabe and Father Mike are going to be here any second."

He grinned at her. "They're here now. And I could convince you to make the time." He brought out the mug of coffee he was holding behind his back. "Instead, I brought you this. Finelli's here, too."

He strode toward the shower and grabbed a quick kiss before he handed her the mug. "Hurry. We need your insights on this."

She had two problems, Cilla thought as she watched him walk toward the door. And she didn't have any insights at all on how to solve the one she was looking at.

THE MEN WERE ALL GATHERED around the flat-screen TV when Cilla joined them. Finelli had brought donuts as well as the file on Elizabeth Baxter. She saw four photos on display. One was the close-up of Elizabeth that Ben had enlarged the night before. Another was one of Elizabeth with her long hair, handing Jonah the green box tied with red ribbon. A third was the photo of Elizabeth that had been taken by the coroner. The fourth was a young man with close-cropped blond hair and the same high forehead and blue eyes that Elizabeth had. It was the photo of Robert Baxter that Gabe had taken from his military file.

"How sure are we that it's the same girl?" Finelli asked, gesturing with his donut at the pictures of Elizabeth.

"Elizabeth Baxter was an army brat," Gabe said. "She and her twin brother, Robert, lost their parents when they were five and the uncle, Paul Baxter, became their guardian. Paul was a career man in the army so they moved around a lot. Spent their high school years in a private boarding school near Colorado Springs. I've got some men on it. They're visiting the school this morning. We may be able to track down dental records through them and identify your Jane Doe."

Finelli waved at the TV screen. "Until we can be sure, I say we go with the theory that our Jane Doe is Elizabeth Baxter. What else do we know?"

"I believe the man who fell off Cilla's fire escape is Sergeant Paul Baxter." Jonah clicked a key on the computer and another image joined those on the screen. "I ran the photo we had from the security discs through military databases during the night and the match was waiting this morning."

"I traced Paul Baxter through more conventional methods," Gabe said. "But I agree with Jonah's ID."

"He sure looks like the guy we've been calling Tank," Finelli said. "We can check his fingerprints to confirm that. His doctors have him in an induced coma because of the head injury he suffered during the fall. They say there is some scarring in the brain because of previous injuries, and it may be days before I can question him."

"That fits with what I learned," Gabe said. "Paul Baxter was trained in explosives, and in Iraq, he worked on a special ops team. He received a medical discharge a year ago when he suffered head injuries in a land-mine explosion."

"That also fits with what he told me yesterday," Cilla said. "He said he was the tactical man and that his partner was the strategic planner. What do we know about the twin brother, Robert?"

"He was honorably discharged from the army a year ago," Gabe said. "That's all I found. Jonah is using his special talents to dig out more details on his military career as we speak."

"You can get into those kinds of records?" Finelli asked.

Jonah smiled.

"You don't want to know the details," Gabe said. "And I have even more interesting news. I've run a quick check, but so far, I can't find any trace of Robert Baxter once he shipped back from Iraq and got his walking papers from the army. No record of taxes filed, no record of employment using that social security number. No death certificate."

"He may have changed his ID," Cilla said. "The uncle changed his, so he may have helped Robert."

"That would be my guess," Gabe agreed. "The bad news is we don't have any idea what name he's operating under now."

"And he's been smart enough to keep in the background and let his uncle do the dirty work. The twin certainly has to be a person of interest, and we have to find him."

"I agree," Finelli said.

Cilla turned to Father Mike. "How long was Elizabeth at the center?"

"Six months," the priest said. "Gabe asked me to check the records. I remember meeting with her and she said that she had just moved to Denver. In the fall, she was going to enroll at the community college. She said that she wasn't Catholic but she enjoyed working with children."

"Robert Baxter was deployed to Iraq at about the same time Elizabeth moved to Denver," Gabe said. "I've got men who are going to check out the community college today and perhaps even track down where she was living in Denver."

"Do we know anything else?" Finelli asked.

Cilla moved closer to the screen and tapped on the green box with the red ribbon. "We can theorize. Twins are close. I'm guessing Elizabeth must have kept Robert fully informed of everything that was going on in her life, including the Christmas present she gave Jonah that year."

"Letters," Father Mike said. "I didn't know her all that well, but she was always carrying a notebook and she would write frequently in it."

"If the first time they were separated was when they left that boarding school, she probably let him know that she was falling in love with Jonah," Cilla said. "Who knows how she told that story in her letters? And what if she told her twin Jonah rejected her, and she'd decided that the best way to eventually be with her true love was to commit suicide? What would that do to you if you received those letters on the other side of the globe and you had no way to get back to her?"

Finelli frowned at the TV screen. "I can buy into your theory so far. But if he's been out a year, why wait to get his revenge?"

"Planning," Jonah said. "And he obviously wants more than to just push me into my next life. He wants some payback first. He's already targeted Cilla—not merely because she's interfered with some of his plans, but also because he's sensed she's important to me. I think he's going to try to target Pleasures also."

"Because it was Pleasures that took you away from Denver," Cilla said. "That has to be why she followed you here to San Francisco and committed suicide here."

"If you're right," Finelli said, "I suggest you shut

down the place until Christmas is over, or until we catch this whack job. Or at least figure out if your theory is correct."

"No," Cilla said.

Everyone turned to her then, but it was Jonah's eyes she met and held. "Shutting down Pleasures could be exactly what he wants. It's December 23, and tonight you're throwing a huge party at Pleasures. I think he'd love to see you cancel it. Number one, you'd annoy the people who've traveled here especially to attend. Number two, you'd lose all those checks that the guests were going to write for the boys and girls clubs here in San Francisco. The club takes a hit. Your favorite charity takes a hit. It's another way of making you suffer before he takes a final run at you on the twenty-fourth."

"I think you're right," Jonah said. "Not only that, I'll bet you when I don't cancel, he finds a way to join the party. He hasn't made a mistake yet. Maybe we can lure him into making one tonight."

"It's going to be a hell of a job to handle the security," Gabe said.

Jonah grinned at him. "You don't think G.W. Securities is up to the job?"

Gabe didn't return the grin, but Cilla could tell he was thinking. "You've already got the security cameras in place. We can use this apartment as our headquarters, and we'll wire you and Cilla." The smile formed slowly. "And I've got a couple of new gadgets we can use."

Jonah turned to Finelli. "We can also use the San Francisco Police Department."

Finelli sighed in defeat. "This could turn into a real Christmas nightmare."

16

THE PARTY AT PLEASURES was a Christmas fantasy come true. From her position at the top of the staircase, Cilla was able to see the expressions on the faces of the guests entering the club. None of them was aware they were using the occasion to trap a would-be killer.

She could also see Jonah standing at the foot of the stairs, greeting everyone as they came in. He looked totally relaxed, smiling and shaking hands as though the Christmas event was the only thing on his mind. Gabe stood next to him so he was safe for now. But her stomach was in knots because she had a feeling that the person behind the notes was indeed going to make an appearance at the party.

And soon. Cilla let her gaze sweep the place again. On the second floor, the tables had been shoved against the wall. Crystal chandeliers glittered overhead. Women in jewel-colored gowns danced with their partners on a gleaming parquet floor while a band played slow tunes in the background.

On the lower floor, drinks were being offered to the arriving guests in the bar, and in the dining room, long tables held an array of food. Silver-and-white trees twinkled in the corners.

Gibbons and Santos were in Jonah's apartment monitoring the surveillance cameras. The wire she was wearing had a remote switch tucked beneath the strap of her dress so that she could turn it off or on. And tucked into a small flower on the same strap was a little video camera that would send close-up pictures of anyone who talked with her.

For the past hour, there'd been no reason to activate either the camera or her mic. Guests had been arriving in a steady stream. She even recognized some of them, including the nightly news anchorwoman who had been dominating Jonah's time for the past ten minutes.

Next year, Cilla was going to make sure Jonah threw a Christmas party that she could enjoy. Sans anchorwoman.

Next year.

As the two words ran through her mind again, Cilla felt her stomach plummet. Somehow in the past few days, a one-night stand she'd been determined to walk away from had morphed into *next year.* Maybe longer? Her stomach pitched again.

She pressed her hand against it and focused on the next group of people coming in the front door.

"Do you need something to eat?"

"I'm fine." Cilla turned to face the pretty brunette who stood beside her. Nicola Guthrie, a special agent with the FBI office in Denver, was also Gabe's fiancée, and Gabe had arranged for her to fly in for the party and assigned her to watch Cilla for the evening. "Just nerves."

Nicola glanced down the staircase to where Jonah stood in the receiving line with Gabe. "Gabe won't let anything happen to Jonah. Nash would be here, too, if his grandmother hadn't arranged that cruise with their new family members."

"Jonah is safe for tonight," Cilla agreed. But it wasn't Christmas Eve yet, and if they weren't able to stop whoever was behind the threat tonight... All day long as they'd waited for Gabe's men to report in on the Baxter twins, she'd been plagued by a growing certainty that time was running out.

And they still had very little to go on. The only thing they now knew for certain was that the body that had washed up six years ago beneath the piers was indeed Elizabeth Baxter.

Gabe's men had been able to contact her advisor and one of her professors at the community college where she'd attended classes. The professor had confirmed her interest in Eastern religions and reincarnation.

All they had on her twin, Robert, was that his teachers at the private boarding school considered him brilliant but subject to drastic mood swings. And they all remarked on how close the twins were, inseparable almost. One of Robert's teachers had encouraged the young man to apply to West Point, but he was too impatient to follow in his uncle's footsteps and serve his country in combat. The guidance counselor described him as borderline genius but with anger issues that at times resulted in drastic changes in personality. The counselor had also remarked on the closeness of the twins.

What Jonah had been able to unearth from Robert's military files didn't shed much further light. Several times he'd been reprimanded for insubordination, but his commanding officer had also reported frequently on his bravery and his aptitude for strategic planning.

Although his advice had been unsolicited at first, the unit had learned to rely on his insights before going on a mission. It would have helped to be able to speak to his commanding officer, but the man had died in Iraq.

"There's so much we don't know," Cilla said. "If our current theory is correct and Elizabeth's twin is behind this, he could wait us out. Maybe he isn't even here. Or he could be here just enjoying the party, and relishing what he has planned for tomorrow. Or if we've rattled him too much, he could make a move on Jonah that we don't stop."

Nicola took her hand and squeezed it. "You'll stop it. Gabe and Jonah and I will help you stop it. We've got every available agent from G.W. Securities here. Your friend Finelli brought quite a few cops, and they have good eyes."

Nicola was right, Cilla told herself. The security was as tight as they could make it. Several of Gabe's agents were circulating on the first floor, and Finelli was all suited up in a white waiter's jacket in the bar.

"Who is that man talking to Jonah right now?" Nicola asked.

Cilla glanced down the stairs. "That's Carl Rockwell. He was one of the original investors in Pleasures and he's one of Jonah's partners in a new club they plan to open in San Diego. Why?"

"For a second, when he smiled at Jonah, he reminded me of someone. But I can't place him."

"I asked Gabe to check him out because his association with Jonah began when he invested in Pleasures. But that was after Christmas." She turned to Nicola. "And you can see I'm grasping at straws. I'm not sure I'm even thinking clearly anymore."

"Jonah is more than a case to you."

Cilla hesitated, then said, "He shouldn't be. I didn't want him to be."

"You've fallen in love with him."

Cilla's stomach dropped as hard and fast as a rock, and panic spewed up to fill the space left behind. "No. Maybe. We haven't known each other long enough. I like him, of course. But I keep telling myself we're just having a…thing. It's just a chemistry thing."

And she was babbling.

"Uh-huh."

"He's… We're…all wrong." But the more she spoke, the greater the panic became.

"That's a sure sign," Nicola said. "That 'all wrong' thing. When I ran into Gabe a few months ago, I thought he was an art thief just like his father. I wanted to arrest him."

"But you didn't."

Nicola grinned at her. "It was a chemistry thing. I decided to jump him instead, and it turned out to be a much better choice. We're getting married in February on Valentine's Day."

Married.

No, she thought. There was no fairy-tale ending for her. She didn't believe in them. That had always been the dream her mother had chased so unsuccessfully. She opened her mouth to say so, and then shut it as Father Mike Flynn started up the stairs toward them. When he reached them, Nicola leaned in to kiss his cheek. "Father Mike, will you keep Cilla company for a minute? I'm going to run down and get us a plate of food."

As soon as Nicola was out of earshot, Cilla said, "I hope you're saying a lot of prayers."

He reached out and took her hand in both of his. "I'm sure you've said quite a few yourself."

"Yes, but sometimes God doesn't answer them the way you'd like him to. My aunt Nancy, who was a nun, always said that sometimes, God just says no. But I understand the statue of St. Francis has some pull. You wouldn't happen to have a direct line to it, would you?"

Father Mike smiled. "I mentioned the situation to him before Gabe picked me up this morning."

Glancing down, Cilla saw Stan and Glenda Rubin enter the club. They had an entourage with them that included Dean Norris as well as Glenda's sister and brother-in-law. When he reached Jonah in the reception line, Stan pulled him into a hug and Jonah returned it. The gesture had her thinking of Jonah's father again.

She turned to Father Mike. "Did Jonah mention to you that he's trying to track down his father?"

Surprise flickered over the priest's face. "No."

"It wasn't his idea. I nagged him into it. When you're working on a case like this, you have to pull on every thread, and you have to look at everyone who might have a motivation. Family always pops to the top of the list."

"Of course," Father Mike said.

"Knowing what we do now, I think it's highly unlikely that his father is involved. Jonah hasn't been able to find any trace of him, not even a death certificate. But he believes that the life Darrell Stone lived in Denver may have been based on an identity he created solely for the purpose of living with his family—for whatever reason. I think he'll keep looking."

"I've never known Jonah to give up once he sets his mind to something." Father Mike gave her hands one final squeeze before he released them. "I can see you care a great deal about him. What I can tell you is that the first part of Jonah's prayer to St. Francis on that long-ago Christmas Eve will be answered."

He turned then and surveyed the partygoers below them. "If Jonah's father hadn't failed to return to his family, Jonah might not be doing the kind of work that he's doing for boys and girls in Denver and here. When the St. Francis Center for Boys had to close down, he was the one who convinced Gabe and Nash to open a new one to include both boys and girls. They put their own money into it."

Another group of guests entered the club.

Glancing down, Father Mike clasped her wrist. "Who is that young man shaking Jonah's hand right now?"

Cilla tensed as her gaze shot to Jonah. "That's Dean Norris. He's a protégé of Stan Rubin, the older man talking to Gabe. Stan is Jonah's new partner for the club he's opening in San Diego. Why do you ask?"

"Maybe nothing. He took his glasses off to wipe them when he arrived. And for a moment, I thought..."

"What?" Cilla pressed. Below her, Dean took a glass of champagne from a passing waiter. Glenda laughed.

With a sigh, Father Mike shook his head. "My eyes are playing tricks on me. Looking at those images of Elizabeth Baxter and her brother on the TV screen for so long this morning brought back memories of when she worked at the center. For just a moment, I thought that young man down there resembled her. But I can see now that he doesn't. I must be getting old."

At that moment, Dean brushed his hair off his forehead, then glanced up at her and waved.

The feeling tingled up her spine.

For just an instant, she thought she caught a hint of

resemblance, too. Not to the image that had been in the old case file, but to one of the photos Ben had shot. Then Dean smiled and the impression faded.

But the feeling didn't. It only grew as he turned to say something to Stan and then started up the stairs toward her. Jonah was already talking to the next arrivals, so there wasn't any time to tell him what she was feeling.

"Father Mike," she spoke in a low voice, "I'm going to get Dean to give you his champagne glass. There'll be fingerprints on it, so guard it with your life until you can get it to Nicola."

"Will do," Father Mike murmured.

"Cilla," Dean said as he reached her. "I was hoping we'd have a chance to chat. I want to apologize for using you to vent yesterday. I was letting my disappointment take control. I tend to do that a bit too often."

"No problem. I'd like you to meet Father Mike Flynn. I was just telling him that you're working with Stan and Jonah on the new club they're opening in San Diego."

Dean held out his free hand. "Father Mike."

The priest grasped it.

While the two men exchanged greetings, she studied Dean. The hair color and eye color were wrong, but when he stood in profile as he did now, her feeling grew even stronger. Elizabeth would be twenty-four now, and that matched her guestimate of how old Dean was. Plus, he'd just been discharged from the military when he'd approached Stan for a job.

But she needed evidence. "Dean, I feel it's such a shame to waste this music. Will you let Father Mike hold your champagne while you dance with me?"

He turned back to her. "I'd love to."

She took his arm and urged him onto the dance floor. If he was Robert Baxter, then the best thing she could do was keep him away from Jonah. And the glass might give them the evidence they needed.

She slipped her finger beneath the flower on her shoulder strap and flicked the switch on the little camera and mic.

They were in the center of the dance floor before Dean turned her into his arms. "I wanted to thank you for what you said to me yesterday. When I know I'm right about something, and others just don't see it, I get impatient."

She looked up and met his eyes. "You get angry."

His grin was a bit sheepish. "I do have a temper. And a bit of an ego problem, I admit. But talking with you made me realize that I *will* see my designs become a reality someday. I just have to be patient."

And the man dancing with her *was* patient. He was the same young man who'd come over to introduce himself in the Rubins' suite. Before he'd become impatient with the children.

"Stan told me that once our San Diego club gets on its feet, he's going to join Carl Rockwell and Jonah to finance that club in Seattle. Then my designs could come to fruition."

As he guided her into a turn, Cilla studied his face. There was none of the tension, none of the barely controlled anger radiating off him that she'd noted when he'd talked about his designs before. It was almost as if this young man and the angry one she'd seen yesterday were two different people.

What if they were? As Dean guided her around the dance floor, her feeling grew stronger. Two people. She turned the idea over in her mind. If Robert Baxter was suffering from some personality disorder, it might explain his guidance counselor's description of him as brilliant at times and childish at others. It might also explain the different reports in his military file. And hadn't she and Jonah believed from the beginning that they were dealing with two people? One an impulsive risk taker, the other a planner? Not Robert and his uncle, but perhaps two Roberts?

Her experience with multiple personalities was limited to old movies—*Sybil* starring Sally Field, and *The Three Faces of Eve* starring Joanne Woodward. But she knew the trick would be to get the other Robert, the angry Robert, to come out.

The music segued into another song.

"One more dance?" she asked. "I know I can't monopolize your whole evening."

"I'd love another dance."

She noted that they were at the far end of the dance floor now, about as far away from Jonah as she could hope for. She'd turned her camera and mic on. As he guided her into a waltz, she tilted her head back and met his eyes. "You must have had a tough time in the military."

The smile wavered. The hand at her waist and the one holding hers both tightened.

"What do you mean? And how did you even know I was in the military?"

"Glenda mentioned your military background to me when you were presenting your ideas for Jonah's approval. And I just meant that having a hair-trigger temper must have been a problem for you when you were in the service."

"It wasn't." The smile was completely gone now, and his tone was defensive. "I was written up for bravery several times. Anger in the army can be channeled toward the enemy. Plus, my commanding officer often complimented me on my ideas on mission strategy."

There was tension radiating off him now, so Cilla decided to go for broke. She sent up a quick prayer that her mic and camera were working and that at least one of her men in Jonah's apartment was paying attention.

"What if I told you that I know who you really are?" she asked.

He missed a step but quickly recovered. "I'm Dean Norris."

"No." She smiled, kept her tone reasonable, friendly. "You're Robert Baxter and your twin sister, Elizabeth, committed suicide here in San Francisco six years ago on Christmas Eve. You want to avenge her death."

"I don't know what you're talking about."

But he did. She saw the flicker of fear in his eyes and the flash of fury before he could mask either. She decided to push again.

"Yes, you do. I worked on Elizabeth's case when she died. I've been looking into it again. You and your sister were close. When you left her to go into the army, she must have been very lonely. She wrote you letters, but I bet you didn't have time to answer all of them. You have to feel some responsibility that she turned to Eastern religions and some cockeyed theory of reincarnation."

He squeezed her wrist so hard that Cilla was surprised she didn't hear bones snap.

"It wasn't cockeyed if Elizabeth believed in it. And I wasn't the person who caused her to commit suicide." The words were a hiss. The breath he drew in was ragged as he blinked his eyes. "She died to be with Jonah Stone."

Cilla felt the hard poke just above her waist.

"You're making me change my plans again and you'll pay. I have a gun in my pocket. You'll do as I say or I'll shoot the people around us."

The look in his eyes told her that he wasn't kidding. She'd gotten just what she'd wanted. The angry childish Robert had come out to play.

He smiled. "And then I'll shoot you. It's not my favorite plan, but Jonah will come, and I'll kill him a day early."

Terror buzzed in her head, but she ignored it. She had to get him away from the crowd. "What do you want me to do?"

"We'll just walk toward the staircase. Jonah is still greeting guests at the bottom."

She swallowed hard and thought. "No. You're not thinking, because you're angry." Her mistake for bringing out the childish Robert. Now she needed the brilliant Robert. "Gabe Wilder, his best friend, is with him. Detective Finelli is in the dining room. They won't let you take him."

He hesitated.

"There's a staircase to the kitchen just a few feet from here. You can take a breath. Think." She had to get him away from the guests, away from Jonah. "If you take me to the staircase, Jonah will come to you."

"Yes. Good." He drew in a breath and let it out. "Go."

THE LINE OF ARRIVALS was finally thinning. Jonah continued to smile and chat, but the feeling was growing that something was going to happen. Soon.

And he was missing something. He'd looked every guest in the eye, shaken every hand. If one of them was

Robert Baxter, he hadn't been able to either see it or sense it.

He let his gaze sweep the dining room, then the bar. But all he could see was people enjoying themselves at a party. Stan Rubin caught his eye and lifted a glass. He wanted to talk after the holidays about financing another club in the Seattle area. It would be an opportunity for Dean Norris to try his hand at design. Glenda was laughing at something her sister was saying.

But Dean Norris wasn't with them. Something akin to panic worked its way up his spine. He glanced around the bar again. No sign of Norris there or in the dining room.

His gut tensed. Norris had the wrong coloring, the wrong hair, but he was the right age, and he'd been in the military. Why hadn't he thought of that before? Sweat pearled on his forehead as he turned to Gabe. "Where's Cilla?"

"Same place she was when you asked a few minutes ago. Top of the stairs with Nicola and Father Mike."

Jonah whirled around and saw Nicola talking to Father Mike. No sign of Cilla. Fear hit him like a punch to the gut. "She's not there. Dean Norris has her."

He no sooner had the words out when Gabe put a hand to his ear. "Gibbons and Santos confirm that. She has her mic and camera on. They're in the back staircase."

Jonah was halfway up the stairs before Gabe grabbed his arm and stopped him. Gabe held out a small earpiece. "Listen. She knows what she's doing. If you rush into that stairwell, he'll panic and shoot her."

While Jonah put the piece on, Gabe used a small mic to talk to his men.

17

As they stepped through the doors to the service staircase, Cilla said a little prayer that they wouldn't run into any of the waiters. One of the Roberts had an iron grip on her upper arm and she could feel the barrel of the gun pressing into her side.

The kitchen would be crowded. Before she let him lead her into it, she wanted to make sure she had the more rational Robert with her. So she stopped short on the steps.

"Keep going." He jabbed the gun into her back.

"Take a minute," she said. "Think it through. Killing Jonah can't be all you wanted out of this."

She had to stall, give Gabe a chance to get their men in place. "You didn't join Stanley Rubins's company and wait a year just to get revenge on Jonah. You must have wanted more."

For three beats he didn't say anything. He wasn't moving, either. But his grip on her upper arm didn't loosen.

"What was your original plan?" she asked.

"I wanted to become what Jonah is and take everything that he's built for himself. When he's dead, I'll convince Stanley to buy his places. One day I'll run them. I'll have it all and Jonah Stone will finally be with Elizabeth."

"You could still have it all. Think about designing that new club in Seattle. Maybe you can still figure out a way to get everything you want. I'm the only person who's standing in your way. You don't have to kill anyone else. You don't have to expose yourself."

She paused, hoping that Gabe would figure out what she was going to do.

"There's an exit door in the kitchen that leads to the alley," she said.

"Yes. We'll go into the kitchen and out through the back exit."

She started to move even before he prodded her with the gun. The kitchen when they entered it was crowded and noisy. Pans clattered, steam hissed, a chef called out orders in some kind of chef talk. She took as much time as she could to weave her way through the waiters and cook staff.

She caught a glimpse of Finelli, a loaded tray in his hands. But there was no sign of Jonah or Gabe. Hopefully, they'd be in the alley already.

She reached for the door handle and fumbled with it. He released her upper arm just long enough to pull the heavy door open. And she had just enough time to get her gun out of her wristlet purse before they stepped outside. She held it down, flat at her side.

The night air was cold, the mist like icy fingers on her bare skin. The sky was dark, the illumination from a streetlight dim, and there was no sign of life as they moved quickly along the back of the building. In the distance the sounds of traffic were not loud enough to drown out their footsteps.

They were nearly at the mouth of the alley, close to a couple of large Dumpsters, when he pulled her to a stop. "I'm going to have to shoot you now so I can get back to the party. If my uncle had completed his mission successfully, I would have taken more time with you."

"You've had quite enough time with her," Jonah said from behind them.

Cilla jerked free of Robert's grip, dropped to the ground and rolled. Several gunshots sounded. One of the bullets came close enough to singe her ear. By the time she got her own gun trained on Robert, he was on his knees gripping his now weaponless hand. It was bleeding. Jonah, Gabe, Finelli and Nicola had him surrounded, their guns drawn.

Beyond them, she saw others pour through the kitchen door into the alley—Virgil was in the lead with Father Mike and Carl Rockwell behind him.

"We got him covered," Gabe said to Jonah. "Why don't you help the lady up?"

Jonah picked her up and held her hard against him. She'd barely gotten her arms around him when he drew back far enough to look into her eyes. He'd nearly lost her. Again.

Grabbing her shoulders, he gave her a hard shake. "Dammit, Cilla, we had a deal. We were partners, and you decided to take on that lunatic by yourself."

She raised her chin. "You were my client. I did my job."

"I heard what you said to him. You invited him to kill you." He gave her another shake.

"He didn't. I wouldn't have let him. You didn't let him."

He dragged her back against him and this time covered her mouth with his. As her taste poured through him, some of the fear inside of him eased.

Someone whistled, others applauded. This time when Jonah drew back, he saw that Finelli was loading Robert Baxter into a patrol car that had pulled into the mouth of the alley.

Gabe moved toward them. "She's right, you know. She did her job. Not only do we have Robert Baxter in custody, but very few people at your party even know what went down. She's the best."

Jonah turned and looked at her. Gabe was right. And she'd been right. She was the best. "We need to talk. Right now I have to tell Glenda and Stan what happened out here."

Then he turned and walked back into Pleasures.

FOR THE NEXT TWO HOURS, Cilla found herself fighting off boredom. Jonah hadn't let her stray far from his side except for the short time he'd spent in his office talking to Glenda and Stan Rubin. Even then, he'd told her to stay put outside his office and he'd asked Gabe to keep her there within sight. And since then, if he wasn't directly at her side, Gabe or Nicola or Father Mike was.

Both Gabe and Nicola flanked her now as Jonah announced the results of the silent raffle that had been going on all evening. Cilla had to stifle a yawn. Now that the excitement was over, she was finding that a Christmas charity event, even at Pleasures, was about as exciting as a silent-movie marathon.

And it wasn't just boredom she was feeling. It was nerves. So far Jonah hadn't spoken even one word directly to her.

Not since he'd looked at her in the alley and said, "We need to talk."

"He's still pissed at me," she said to Gabe.

"He nearly lost you. It'll take some time for him to come to terms with that."

"I just did my job."

"Exactly," Nicola said. "And he knows that."

"I'm not sure what to do next."

"I may have an idea for you there," Gabe said. "I found something interesting when I ran the background checks you asked for on the original backers for Pleasures. Then we focused in on the Baxters and I put it aside."

Cilla felt that tingling feeling again. "What did you find?"

"Carl Rockwell worked for various government agencies up until his retirement six years ago. But everything he did is classified. I would have pushed further if I hadn't had to focus on the Baxters. Jonah will be able to find more."

Cilla turned to look at Carl, who was talking to Father Mike. "And he's been backing Jonah's investments ever since he retired from secret government work."

Gabe nodded. "That's what I thought was interesting. You might want to mention it to Jonah."

She looked at Gabe and Nicola. "The two of you stay right here. I'm going to mention it to Carl."

Striding across the room, she made excuses to Father Mike and then drew Carl with her to Jonah's office. Once they were inside, she closed the door and gestured him into a chair. Then she came right to the point. "Why did you leave Jonah and his mother twenty years ago and never come back?"

Carl focused his eyes on her. "Well, you don't beat around the bush, do you?"

No denial. Cilla sat on the edge of Jonah's desk and regarded him steadily. "No. Maybe you should stop beating around the bush and answer my question."

Carl raised his hands to his face and rubbed his fingers against his eyes in a gesture so like Jonah that her heart tightened.

"I've just been having this same conversation with Father Mike."

"Why didn't you come back?" Cilla pressed. "That's the question Jonah's going to ask you."

He glanced up, met her eyes. "I couldn't. The op I was working on went on longer than it was supposed to. Then it went south. I was injured badly. When I woke up, I found myself in a hospital. Years had passed. I'd spent nearly four of them in a coma, and at some point I'd had to have some reconstruction done on my face."

"Why didn't you come back then?"

"I did. I found out where he was and I read the accident reports on my wife's death. I went to Father Mike first, and I was supposed to meet him that evening in the little prayer garden next to the St. Francis Center. I was just outside when Jonah screamed a prayer that he wanted to kill me."

Cilla pictured it in her mind, the man standing in the shadows, the angry boy screaming that he wanted his father back so he could kill him.

"I'd failed both my wife and my son. The life of adventure I'd been leading had been more important to me than they were."

"So you walked away again," she said.

There was pain in his expression. "I went back to the life I was good at. The life that I hadn't been able to give up even when I fell in love, even when I had my son. I wasn't supposed to be married. I created the identity of Darrell Stone because I didn't want the government to know that I had a family. I didn't deserve Jonah. And look what he's made of his life."

Cilla studied the man in front of her. The truth was he'd finally come back into Jonah's life and supported him. And it hadn't taken much trouble on Gabe's part to find information on Carl Rockwell that would raise questions for anyone looking for a connection.

"Well, are you going to walk away again or are you going to tell him?"

"How can he forgive me when I can't forgive myself?"

"You've known him pretty well for six years. If you want the answers to your questions, I'd say Christmas is the best time to get them. The decision is yours."

When Carl said nothing, she pushed it further. "I can tell you one thing. He's looking for you, and knowing Jonah, he'll find you. There's a lot to be said for making a preemptive strike."

HOURS LATER, WHEN PLEASURES was finally dark, Jonah led Cilla up the stairs to his apartment, and with each step, he felt the nerves in his stomach tighten. The evening had gone by in a blur, which had kept those minutes while Cilla had been at the mercy of that lunatic from replaying in his mind. But his duties as host had also prevented him from getting things settled with Cilla.

Stan and Glenda were going to be all right. The shock of what he'd had to tell them about Dean Norris/Robert Baxter had taken its toll. They'd started to think of him as the son they'd never had. But they were going to hire an attorney for him, and Glenda had hugged Jonah before they'd left, thanking him for the idea.

When he opened the door of his apartment, for one moment he entertained the idea of just closing it, pushing her up against it and taking her just as he'd done in that hotel room in Denver. Maybe it would ease the tension inside of him.

But it wouldn't solve the problem of what he was going to say to her. And why didn't he know what to say? He always knew exactly what to say to get what he wanted.

Dammit. No woman had ever succeeded in tying his tongue into knots before.

He just needed a few more minutes, he told himself as he pushed the door shut and strode down the length of the room.

Jonah was still pissed. Maybe Cilla could understand it, but he had to understand her. Flash jumped off her favorite window seat and followed him into the kitchen area. Two against one was not fair. And recalling what she'd said to Carl Rockwell about a preemptive strike, she strode after him.

"You said we needed to talk."

"We do," he said as he pulled a bottle of champagne out of the refrigerator.

She climbed onto a stool and faced him across the counter that separated the kitchen area from the rest of the space. "I'd do it all over again."

"What?"

"Push Robert Baxter into admitting what he'd done, and then getting him out of Pleasures."

"I know you'd do that again. That's who you are." He drew two glasses out of a cabinet, then began to uncork the bottle.

A little bubble of panic formed in Cilla's stomach.

She couldn't get a handle on what he was thinking. Why couldn't she do that?

He poured champagne into the glasses and handed her one.

"We're celebrating?"

"I certainly hope so." He lifted his glass and tapped it against hers. "To the conclusion of a job well-done."

"Done?"

"You're no longer my bodyguard. I'm no longer your client or your partner."

A mix of fear and anger shot through her. Was he going to drop her flat after all she'd done, after everything he'd made her feel?

Over her dead body.

She set her glass down with a loud click and leaned forward. "I have a proposition for you."

"You do?"

"The job may be done, but I want to continue the partnership. I want to move in here."

As the words stopped his ability to breathe, something inside Jonah eased. This was Cilla talking. He took a sip of his champagne and studied her, simply enjoying the sight of her sitting at the counter in his kitchen. In the long nights they'd been apart, he hadn't pictured her here.

She frowned at him. "Well? What do you say?"

"Why do you want to move in here?"

"You allow cats and Flash has grown attached to you."

He sipped his champagne. "Any other reasons?"

"I'll be closer to the office."

His brows rose and he nearly laughed. "A whole three blocks closer. How about the real reason, Cilla?"

She narrowed her eyes on him and frowned. "Okay.

Here it is. I don't want to spend any more nights without you."

He looked at her and saw everything he'd ever wanted. And he was going to hold on to it. To her. Setting his glass down, he held out his hand. When she took it, he gripped hard. "Just one modification. Once you move in here, you're stuck. You stay. I don't want to spend any more nights without you, either."

Smiling, she crawled up and over the counter to wrap herself around him. "When it comes to sticking, I'm the best."

"I'm counting on it," Jonah said as he lowered his mouth to hers.

Epilogue

New Year's Eve...almost midnight

"It's nearly time." Jonah filled the last champagne flute on the tray, then set the bottle down on his kitchen counter.

"This will be the first time I've ever toasted in the New Year with Cristal," Cilla said.

Behind them, guests chattered, and the large TV screen played a delayed broadcast of the partyers in Times Square awaiting the descent of the glittering ball.

Jonah met her eyes as he handed her one of the flutes. "It's a special night, one I want you to remember."

She smiled at him slowly. "I have no trouble at all remembering each and every night I spend with you." There'd been eleven of them so far, and she didn't intend to stop counting.

Virgil joined them at the counter. "Let me do that." Taking the tray, he strode away to serve the rest of the small group in Jonah's apartment.

A much larger party, a bash in fact, was going on below them in Pleasures, but Jonah had invited a few people up to his place to toast the New Year. Gabe, Nicola and Father Mike had returned to Denver on Christmas Eve, but the rest of the people in the room had all played some role in what had happened the night that Robert Baxter was shot and taken into custody in the alley.

Virgil offered flutes of champagne first to the Rubins. They'd extended their stay at the St. Francis Hotel so they could make arrangements for Robert Baxter's defense. Carmen had brought her two sons, and T.D. had brought his pretty wife. Carl Rockwell laughed at something T.D.'s wife was saying.

Carl hadn't waited until Christmas day. He'd visited Jonah's apartment on Christmas Eve. Just in the nick of time as it turned out, because Jonah had been working on his computer most of the afternoon. Cilla figured another day and Carl might have missed his chance to make a preemptive strike. She'd left them alone so she didn't know all they'd talked about that day, but when Carl left, Jonah hugged him and Carl had held on.

"I'm glad Carl's here," she said.

"Me, too. He's my partner, and we've been good friends for a while. Lots of fathers and sons aren't friends. Gabe and Nash don't have their fathers anymore. Carl and I can't get back the years we missed, but we have a future to share."

"Five minutes until the ball drops," Ben called out.

Jonah took her hand as she started toward the TV. "I have something to ask you before we join them."

When she turned back to him, she saw that he had a small box in his hand. When he opened it, all she could do was stare.

It held a ring, and it was so beautiful it made her blink. Something fluttered right under her heart. Panic.

"I know we have an agreement—no more nights apart," Jonah said. "And I know it's a big step, but I want to make what we have definite. Permanent."

The panic fluttered again. And she couldn't quite get a full breath. She thought of her mother and how many times she'd walked down the aisle. Nothing was permanent. Maybe if she could just stop looking at the ring, the panic would stop. She'd be able to breathe. Think.

But when she turned, she found herself facing a group of people and several of them had warned her not to hurt Jonah. It was Carl's look that held hers for a long moment. He raised his glass to her. And she remembered what Jonah had said. *We can't get back the years we missed. But we have a future to share.*

"Cilla?"

Turning back, she looked into his eyes and saw what she wanted. A future to share with Jonah Stone.

Certainty replaced the panic. "Well, are you going to ask me?"

"That's my Cilla." Grinning, Jonah lifted her off her feet and swung her around. "Marry me?"

"I will."

Putting her back down, Jonah slipped the ring on her finger.

"Happy New Year!" Everyone in the room raised their glasses and cheered.

* * * * *

PASSION

For a spicier, decidedly hotter read—
this is your destination for romance!

Harlequin *Blaze*

COMING NEXT MONTH
AVAILABLE DECEMBER 27, 2011

#657 THE PHOENIX
Men Out of Uniform
Rhonda Nelson

#658 BORN READY
Uniformly Hot!
Lori Wilde

#659 STRAIGHT TO THE HEART
Forbidden Fantasies
Samantha Hunter

#660 SEX, LIES AND MIDNIGHT
Undercover Operatives
Tawny Weber

#661 BORROWING A BACHELOR
All the Groom's Men
Karen Kendall

#662 THE PLAYER'S CLUB: SCOTT
The Player's Club
Cathy Yardley

REQUEST YOUR FREE BOOKS!
2 FREE NOVELS PLUS 2 FREE GIFTS!

❦ Harlequin *Blaze*

red-hot reads!

YES! Please send me 2 FREE Harlequin® Blaze™ novels and my 2 FREE gifts (gifts are worth about $10). After receiving them, if I don't wish to receive any more books, I can return the shipping statement marked "cancel." If I don't cancel, I will receive 6 brand-new novels every month and be billed just $4.49 per book in the U.S. or $4.96 per book in Canada. That's a saving of at least 14% off the cover price. It's quite a bargain. Shipping and handling is just 50¢ per book in the U.S. and 75¢ per book in Canada.* I understand that accepting the 2 free books and gifts places me under no obligation to buy anything. I can always return a shipment and cancel at any time. Even if I never buy another book, the two free books and gifts are mine to keep forever.

151/351 HDN FEQE

Name	(PLEASE PRINT)

Address	Apt. #

City	State/Prov.	Zip/Postal Code

Signature (if under 18, a parent or guardian must sign)

Mail to the **Reader Service**:
IN U.S.A.: P.O. Box 1867, Buffalo, NY 14240-1867
IN CANADA: P.O. Box 609, Fort Erie, Ontario L2A 5X3

Not valid for current subscribers to Harlequin Blaze books.

Want to try two free books from another line?
Call 1-800-873-8635 or visit www.ReaderService.com.

* Terms and prices subject to change without notice. Prices do not include applicable taxes. Sales tax applicable in N.Y. Canadian residents will be charged applicable taxes. Offer not valid in Quebec. This offer is limited to one order per household. All orders subject to credit approval. Credit or debit balances in a customer's account(s) may be offset by any other outstanding balance owed by or to the customer. Please allow 4 to 6 weeks for delivery. Offer available while quantities last.

Your Privacy—The Reader Service is committed to protecting your privacy. Our Privacy Policy is available online at www.ReaderService.com or upon request from the Reader Service.

We make a portion of our mailing list available to reputable third parties that offer products we believe may interest you. If you prefer that we not exchange your name with third parties, or if you wish to clarify or modify your communication preferences, please visit us at www.ReaderService.com/consumerschoice or write to us at Reader Service Preference Service, P.O. Box 9062, Buffalo, NY 14269. Include your complete name and address.

HB11B

*Brittany Grayson survived a horrible ordeal at the hands
of a serial killer known as The Professional...
who's after her now?*

*Harlequin® Romantic Suspense presents a new installment
in Carla Cassidy's reader-favorite miniseries,*
LAWMEN OF BLACK ROCK.

Enjoy a sneak peek of
TOOL BELT DEFENDER.

*Available January 2012
from Harlequin® Romantic Suspense.*

"**B**rittany?" His voice was deep and pleasant and made
her realize she'd been staring at him openmouthed through
the screen door.

"Yes, I'm Brittany and you must be..." Her mind suddenly went blank.

"Alex. Alex Crawford, Chad's friend. You called him
about a deck?"

As she unlocked the screen, she realized she wasn't
quite ready yet to allow a stranger inside, especially a male
stranger.

"Yes, I did. It's nice to meet you, Alex. Let's walk around
back and I'll show you what I have in mind," she said. She
frowned as she realized there was no car in her driveway.
"Did you walk here?" she asked.

His eyes were a warm blue that stood out against his
tanned face and was complemented by his slightly shaggy
dark hair. "I live three doors up." He pointed up the street to
the Walker home that had been on the market for a while.

"How long have you lived there?"

"I moved in about six weeks ago," he replied as they

walked around the side of the house.

That explained why she didn't know the Walkers had moved out and Mr. Hard Body had moved in. Six weeks ago she'd still been living at her brother Benjamin's house trying to heal from the trauma she'd lived through.

As they reached the backyard she motioned toward the broken brick patio just outside the back door. "What I'd like is a wooden deck big enough to hold a barbecue pit and an umbrella table and, of course, lots of people."

He nodded and pulled a tape measure from his tool belt. "An outdoor entertainment area," he said.

"Exactly," she replied and watched as he began to walk the site. The last thing Brittany had wanted to think about over the past eight months of her life was men. But looking at Alex Crawford definitely gave her a slight flutter of pure feminine pleasure.

Will Brittany be able to heal in the arms of Alex, her hotter-than-sin handyman…or will a second psychopath silence her forever? Find out in
TOOL BELT DEFENDER
Available January 2012
from Harlequin® Romantic Suspense
wherever books are sold.

Chapter 50

KILMARTIN WAS FIDGETY, and he had a cowed, expectant look to him. The new clothes he had taken so much trouble to pick out just didn't work. The cut of the jacket, the pattern on the shirt, looked way too full of effort, and the shoes looked downright uncomfortable. He cleared his throat, and turned up toward the restaurant with Minogue.

"A stone cold killer they call them," he said. "The FBI."

Minogue had almost forgotten the course that Kilmartin had taken years ago in Virginia.

"They profile them, they dissect them – in a manner of speaking now – and they do a thousand interviews with them, but they're still a what you call it, a…"

"Enigma?"

"That's the word. Puzzle, we'll call it."

"I heard they gave him four transfusions no less. Four. All those donations, just to keep him alive. And for what?"

The old Kilmartin was revving up, all right, Minogue noted.

"As for the other fella, well he wasn't as quick on his feet as he should have been, was he."

With eyes almost clenched shut, Minogue

had taken a fleeting glance at the other man lying awkwardly between a chair and the table. The dark mass above his scalp was blood and something else Minogue didn't want to know about.

Kilmartin seemed to be walking slower on purpose. They came to Wicklow Street. The Chang's restaurant was within sight now. The deal was that Kathleen would bring Maura Kilmartin earlier.

"A shame about that poor divil though," Kilmartin said. "That Fanning fella that got mixed up with them. Never knew what hit him, I suppose."

Minogue was a little tempted to ask Kilmartin if he felt a bit sorry for the Murphy character, the one awaiting positive identification from the car.

"And then to just dump him, and the car of course – on top of a car he dumped earlier on. What kind of a man can do that, I say to myself. What kind of a human being. ... But why should I think that. God knows, we met enough of them over the years. Didn't we?"

Kilmartin had been talking non-stop since they had parked.

"And another thing," Kilmartin went on. "There's no way around this: it dehumanizes people. The army, I'm talking about. Any army. Put a man in a uniform, give him a gun, let him think he's better than the people he's looking at, and that's what you're going to get – oh, and keep him ignorant, of course, so he's sure of himself and doesn't be thinking too hard about what he's ordered to do."

Minogue did not want to dip his toes in that one.

"But who's responsible in the final analysis, I say."

"For what?"

"What that fella did, or those fellas did. Out there in Iraq, I'm saying. By the way, don't take this the wrong way, but your listening skills are not up to scratch."

Minogue gave him the eye.

"It's true," said Kilmartin. "You know it. Sorry to say, but."

Straight from the Self-Help section, Minogue wanted to retort. He began to make up titles for what Kilmartin had read, or consulted. Spousal Bliss Through Listening to Your Life Partner. Ears of Love. Tantric Listening.

"He should have turned in that other fella," Kilmartin said. "When he found he was dealing over there. 'West Ham' or whatever his name was."

"Parker. Gary Parker."

"No sense of right and wrong when you're in the army. And sure the world knows, you can't deal with a junkie. Not one inch can you trust one. But there he is, covering up for this fella over there in Iraq. That's not how to do things, is it."

"Hardly."

"The story I heard," Kilmartin said, his voice dropping. "I heard a rumour they were, em, gay."

"Em gay, or just gay?"

"There you go again. But did you hear that too?"

"I heard nothing."

"I thought gay fellas were supposed to be, you know?"

"So did I."

"I'm just saying that it's not the stereo-type."

Minogue said nothing.

"So here's this fella, a corporal, and he's trying to shield the other fella. And then see what happens for his trouble – your man goes off the deep end one night, and that family there in Iraq winds up dead. Isn't that it? Tell me that's an accident now."

"Not in the record," said Minogue, the urge to mischief returning. He thought of Kathleen's injunction, and the promise she had extracted from him, to try to avoid rows tonight.

"Ah stop it, would you? The army brass got them out of there so fast, whitewashed the proceedings. Like they do everywhere, the British. Oh yes. Some people may forget, but the Irish don't."

"Don't forget what?"

"Are you going to tell me it's okay for some freelance hit men, trained and primed over in England, to be let loose here in Ireland?"

"Our gangsters hired them."

"And what does that prove?"

Minogue looked up and down Wicklow Street. It was still one of his favourite steets of all in the city. The curve as it slid down toward Grafton Street beckoned him always, its trove of side streets like adventures of their own.

Kilmartin made a sour laugh then.

"Wonder who gave those other fellas the tip-off," he said. "I say it was Egan himself. The kind of thing the bastard would do. Save him having to pay them."

Minogue couldn't disagree. Malone had told him that the word was West Ham had gotten out of hand at an after-hours in Finglas, and blathered about what they did, and what they could do. He waited until Kilmartin took a pause.

"James. James?"

"What. What are you Jamesing me for?"

Minogue looked at his friend, took in the fierce eyebrow slant, the blinking.

"James. You're just blathering. It's too much. Okay?"

Kilmartin made to say something but held back. A look of desperation crossed his face for a moment, but was quickly gone.

"Easy for you," he said, quietly.

Minogue did not think so. Nor did he think he could ever tell his friend how much he had tried to dissuade Kathleen from doing this.

"Look," said Kilmartin, nudging his arm. "It's like I told Herlighy. That old goat, sure he's gone deaf, I'm sure. 'I want what I had,' I says to him when he asks me where I wanted to be when this was over. 'Well you won't have that,' he says. 'Nobody can have that.' Something about the same river twice?"

"Not as deaf as you think then, is he. Or as dumb."

"Whisht, will you. Says he, things are not just going to happen – what's the word he used? To ensue. Big word. You have to write the script, practise your role and then produce the film, says he. Or the play – I was going to say 'drama' but by Jesus, I don't want to use that word, do I."

Minogue nodded. The thought of the Szechuan noodles had cheered him a little.

"It's just a dinner," he said to Kilmartin.

"For you it is. For me, it's auditioning."

"Just keep it light, that's the trick."

"No mention of why she tried to kill herself then, I suppose."

Minogue stared at him. Too far gone? Maybe he had misjudged Kilmartin entirely.

Maybe the silent bitterness ran deeper and longer than even Kilmartin himself knew.

"Well you got that out of your system at least," he said.

Kilmartin sighed and shuffled his coat.

"I don't know why I said that."

"You're nervous. But I'm going to kick you under the table if I think that class of a comment is on its way out of your mouth again."

Kilmartin examined the cement edges of the footpath. He let out a deep breath. He looked up then, his face easing a little.

"Did you say a kick, or a tap under the table?"

"A kick I said. I'll root you out of it, so I will."

Kilmartin nodded as though to agree.

"And you're certain she doesn't know?" he asked.

"Not unless you told her."

Almost against his wishes, a small smile of satisfaction crept over Kilmartin's features. He looked across at the restaurant window.

"I don't much like Chinese food," he said.

"Ask them for potatoes and cabbage instead, why don't you."

"I don't want any trouble from you. Kathleen I like, but you, you're work."

"You behave yourself in there. You Mayo bullock."

"Listen to you. A mucker from Clare. I'll have to show you how to use a knife and fork again, I suppose."